After All!

Other volumes in *Hugh Hood: The Collected Stories*

Hugh Hood

After All!

THE COLLECTED STORIES

V

The Porcupine's Quill

NATIONAL LIBRARY OF CANADA CATALOGUING IN PUBLICATION DATA

Hood, Hugh, 1928–2000
After all! : the collected stories V/Hugh Hood.

ISBN 0-88984-258-2

I. Title.

PS8515.O49A74 2003   C813'.54   C2003-901829-6
PR9199.3.H59A74 2003

1 2 3 4 • 05 04 03

Published by The Porcupine's Quill,
68 Main Street, Erin, Ontario NOB 1TO.
www.sentex.net/˜pql

Readied for the press by W. J. Keith; copy edited by Doris Cowan.
Typeset in Galliard, printed on Zephyr Antique laid,
and bound at the Porcupine's Quill.

Represented in Canada by the Literary Press Group.
Trade orders are available from University of Toronto Press.

We acknowledge the support of the Ontario Arts Council,
and the Canada Council for the Arts for our publishing program.
The financial support of the Government of Canada
through the Book Publishing Industry Development Program
is also gratefully acknowledged. Thanks, also, to the Government of
Ontario through the Ontario Media Development Corporation's
Ontario Book Initiative.

 Canada Council
for the Arts
Conseil des Arts
du Canada

 Canadä

 ONTARIO ARTS COUNCIL
CONSEIL DES ARTS DE L'ONTARIO

Table of Contents

Foreword

After All! contains the last of Hugh Hood's short stories, seventeen in all, written between September 1991 and December 1994. It was his practice to intersperse publication of short stories, essays, or other materials between the appearance of the individual novels in his ambitious series *The New Age / Le Nouveau siècle*, which appeared at two- or three-year intervals between 1975 and 2000. This collection should have been published in 1996 or 1998, but because of failing health in the later 1990s, he devoted all his energies to the completion of the *New Age* series, and thus never got around to presenting the typescript to a publisher. (Hood died, sadly, a few weeks before the publication of the final volume of the *New Age* series.) The stories in this collection, however, are not only complete in themselves but complete *as a collection*. They are presented in the order in which they were written, which was the order in which he wanted them to appear.

Like his earlier collections (from *Flying a Red Kite*, 1962, onwards), these stories encompass a remarkable variety of tones. They include humorous stories of everyday life, fantasies, problem stories, satires on the excesses of modern civilization, documentary sketches, stories that amuse, stories that entertain, stories that set one thinking, stories that disturb. All are written with the stylistic elegance, and filled with the inquiring intelligence, that we have come to expect from him. Though written in the last decade of his life, they show him at the top of his form. Here we experience the flowering of one of the most skilful and probing Canadian practitioners of the short story as a subtle and concentrated literary form.

– *W. J. Keith*, 2002

Bit Parts

After that he began to turn up from time to time, at first in small bits, the sole of his shoe or an elbow-patch. A narrow expanse of ugly green tweed, the collar of a light fall topcoat, a long leg. She had to assemble him slowly, putting together the information as it came. She never had a full range of vision in her dreams. There was always a surrounding darkness at the edges.

When she was asleep she couldn't be certain that her dreams were in colour. Afterwards it seemed to her that they were; she could always say, a green tweed coat, a brown leather patch, but she might have imagined these details after the fact. How could she be sure that she was dreaming? Well, for one thing, the indistinct curving frame was never in evidence when she was awake. And there were other signs.

It was not like a movie.

Unless like an old black-and-white movie on a narrow screen.

People – unrecognizable extras – came and went in the background.

A collar, a leg.

She started to have unfamiliar sensations, asleep and awake, feelings of being pulled, tugged, of flowing, a drift.

This happened mostly when she was awake. She might be going along her own street, leaving her apartment or coming home, when a thrusting impulse would lay hands on her. Unclarified impulses vaguely, then sharply received. This was when he began to be visible full-length. In colour or in black-and-white? She could tell what colour hair he had but she couldn't exactly see it while he was moving in the dream. He did the usual things.

He was adept at pouring out drinks and handing around bits of cheese on wafers. Certain noises were characteristic, his shoes on the thick carpet, humming of a song she knew well, not always the same song, but the same voice.

Different dreams had different stories: sometimes she was

crossing Europe in a small car, headed for some Balkan capital, when all at once he would appear dressed as a border-crossing inspector, oddly-shaped kepi, silver buttons. Or as an Orthodox priest with a funny biretta. Head-coverings were important for some reason. Once she glimpsed him at a distance in some Olympic stadium, costumed as an undercover security agent. She could tell him by his silenced gun.

There is a sound such a gun produces. *Shhsst. Pffffft.* Then the surprised look and the slow fall.

At this stage he began to turn up full-length, half concealed in a doorway, crossing a corridor. He was never the star or a featured player; these were bit parts but somehow more important in proportion to their insignificance than the longer roles of the stars.

Doorman, security man, roadie, groupie, beggarman.

In daylight on the streets she felt pushed and invited; things happened on buses, bumpings.

He had a line of dialogue in a major dream. 'If you would come this way, Madam.'

She went in fear of his longer parts. How would they develop?

Now when she woke up she dressed at once and left the building in search of something; the thrust around her grew insistent. Somebody was dreaming her.

Finally they met. What an anticlimax! He moved in next door, into Apartment 1904; the man next door. How could she ignore him? All this time she had been playing tiny parts in his dreams. They understood this at once. Interplayers. Midnight walkers.

Now they saw each other full-length, shoes, socks. She started to wear more expensive pantyhose because he might spot the cheap ones, and he pulled up his socks. She suspected that he now wore bikini briefs. This suspicion was partly confirmed by a scene in a dream where they met in the sub-basement laundry-room. They were feeding adjacent dryers and needed loonies for the coin slots. That was their first joint dream; he dreamt about her in Apartment 1904 and she dreamt about him in Apartment 1902. They were growing close.

If you dream all the time about somebody else, and that somebody dreams you, there is only one way to resolve such intimacy.

They began to have that dream that we have all had. Sitting alone in the breakfast nook right next to the wall that separated the two apartments and there would come a shock or thud like the impulse of a nearby earthquake. Slowly at first and then quite quickly the paint would flake off the dividing wall, a hole appear, the substance of the wall crumble, and behold, there was another complete mirror-image apartment on the other side. The dreamer would then step through the now sizeable gap in the wall to find the other person, surprised in the act of lifting toast to parted lips. There came a marmalade-flavoured kiss.

Living together proved the way out.

They moved to a single, much larger apartment in the same building, on the tenth floor, Apartment 1001. L-shaped living/dining area, bathroom, vestibule, powder-room, three bedrooms. Balcony opening off the living area with a northerly view. At first they shared a bedroom but found that this kept them awake. When they finally fell asleep their joint dreams were confused and obscured. Reality drove out fantasy. There was no pleasure to be had from watching the other dressing or undressing. Too explicit.

The fun was in the fantasy.

When you are that close together you can check the accuracy of your lover's dream narrative because you are in it. She dreams that the floor-covering is indigo, flocked, wall-to-wall, smelling of dye. He authenticates this and adds a detail: when you lie on it you can smell acid in the dustballs.

You were wearing Walk-On-Air Joggers.

And you were wearing a Benetton jersey top.

You had been eating fries with vinegar.

And you had belly rumbles from dieting.

Such sharing is the perfection of love, you decide. You inhabit a shared fantastic space, move in the same shadowy spaces, share wishes, inseparable ambitions. You want what is most intense for one another, not what is best. This continues for ages. At last a change begins to show itself. Your ambitions, fantasies, stay strong, filled with impulse; his begin to slow and weaken. You go on wanting the same things but the intensity is only half there. You go to sleep in adjoining bedrooms and the spaces fuse as soon as you fall asleep; you drift into his space and he is slow to react.

He starts using the basin and toilet in the powder-room. You can't get in there, awake or asleep.

He is concealing something. It is like trying to rescue a man over-board. You dive after him; you have to support his weight in the fluid element. His head lolls, goes under. He can swim but chooses not to. The weight becomes unbearable and to save yourself you have to let go. He slides away and you soon lose sight of him in sur-face-level mist. When you wake up he is gone forever.

Dreams to black.

Long delicious sleeps.

Then a slow waking, still dreaming, merging of waking/dream-ing. Very long empty vistas sharply defined in magnificent green and diamond white, gradually filling with sunlight like a day on the north slope of Ellesmere Island. Crystalline, clear, unpeopled, stria-tions of green faults running through the hardest ice, a long sun-shine but a short summer.

Life after man.

Now you can tell when you are awake by familiar landmarks never glimpsed in the high arctic of dream. There aren't the deathly hard whites and greens, only perspectives of grey and black, far-off cityscapes, miniature shopping centres, subways, overpasses, and after some time the sight of automobiles crowding the city. There is the smoke of exhaust, cars buzzing around encircling you, no people visible in the vehicles.

Half life has emptied itself out. When you come home tired and without appetite, unable to zap the package in the microwave, only one action suggests itself before bed. Clear out the empty rooms, prepare to move, dust off the piles of shared belongings, decide which to throw away. Here's an ugly smelly green tweed fall topcoat. Out it goes. It was part of the furniture of sleep. Here's an old jacket. Here's a pile of torn jeans, a Vuarnet T-shirt. Out.

You notice that the atmosphere is now unconditional, still, arid, airless, without currents or invisible impulses in a given direction, your body floating in a void, barely moving, up, down, a sense of regressing to beginnings. Why make a move?

Existence without impulse. Time for bed.

In your sleep a clouded void, clouds like ground mist in twilight, here and there the form of a shrub or tree, the sense of the pathway, awareness of muscles contracting and relaxing, motion towards. Walking. Going for a walk. Innocent words. The right leg moves easily in its supple hip joint. Then the left. Muscles contract causing motion. Eyes strain through the ground mist with a sense of possible horizons, the hint of new distances. The mist is agitated, the quality of the light changes. Can it be morning so soon? Coming out to a wide empty prospect stretching immeasurable distances in the wrong direction. You have not wished to come here, no impulse has directed you, no push between the shoulders, tug from in front. The low horizon defines the bottom third of the picture; an enormous unqualified sky fills out the rest; there are no birds, no people, no cars, no city, unqualified consciousness, pure animation.

No corners here; everything spreads away in all directions without lines or markers, almost without distinction between land and sky. You can tell the land by the sound. Something is grassy, something at the bottom of the surrounding space is ground. Very faintly the sound moves in the grass   whish   whush   whish   whoosh waves. Air moving. Impossible to see air moving. Feeling of something crawling across the forehead, scent of air in wind, how emptiness feels on the breast. Here here nowhere but here.

Awake or asleep every moment when I'm deep in a dream of you in a dream of you of you of you you you.

A given direction?

An empty scape, a voided world. She totters like a boxer with a damaged brain stem. Speech becomes ineffective, throaty, unnecessary. What is seen defines interior absence, wide, dun-coloured, brumous, perhaps endless, even the indistinct crowds have faded from the scene under the unformed heavens.

Late in time she retreats from the breadth of unformed happenstance and moves inside, shrinks into rest, new sleep. The edges form again, the round limits of the imagined picture. Iris in! Into a wash of undisturbed sleep. No more dreaming. Dreams are the harbingers of the future and there is no future for her. She is free of wants now, and neither sees nor hears, just lies by herself.

Report lapses here. How to describe the undifferentiated? The indescribable. Even the blind have sight behind their eyelids, impressions of sparks or purple stripings. She has none, as though the optic nerve has been severed for good and all. No colour and no motion agitate her ease, indescribable, unspeakable, for a long long time, until one night.

Flick.

Whisk.

The sense of new corners and angles of concealment. Something playing hide and seek with her awareness. Some fugitive nicker of animal alarm. She hears faint sounds in her alien sleep. Sounds without assignable intention, quiet whistles, brushing noises, signals of differences, the birth of emotion. In sleep she has wants, rolls on her side, feels the shoulder muscles cramp and wakes, or seems to wake. She rises. Goes to the window or to the encircling iris of her personal camera eye. Looks through the pane at what is there. New differences, creases in the prairie, ripples, unfamiliar articulations of the scape, a place, someplace. Feeling follows form.

Texture mediates being.

The floor of this new scape feels like some sort of fabric, flocking, carpet, mini-tufted stuff. What she senses isn't out of doors. Here comes new light. Whisk. Flick. Whoosh. Motion. Sight. A wide prospect of happiness. Felicity is a peninsula projecting out of life, Europe populated by Asia, by absence.

That green tweed again. Sole of a jogging shoe cracked or split at its widest. Bit of an elbow patched against the cold.

Powerful impulses at her back at the window. Window? The wall has a hole in it. On the impulse she steps through into a new place and is wrapped around by push, shove, tug, impressions of drawnness, of being persuaded on. He is   oh   he is dreaming. Her. He dreams her.

From where? From where?

Assault of the Killer Volleyballs

(For Barry Wainwright)

Mother heard the sound from the attic first, a rhythmic spong-ing noise, insistent and impossible to identify, a rebounding bonking agglomeration of thumps. A sound that might be made by an Airedale trapped in a bass drum. This happened at dawn on a Monday morning when everybody was still asleep.

'Go and see what that is!'

'Why me?'

'Go on, and don't wake the kids. I need another hour before they start to bug me. I haven't made their lunches yet.'

Dad went into the hall and listened. There certainly was something unusual going on up there. The house, an obsolete, post-war, storey-and-a-half affair, had one of those seldom-used top floors only reachable by a counterweighted flight of steps that folded into the ceiling and had to be hauled down towards the floor by a stout cord. Dad was in the act of freeing the cord from the cleat to which the running end was attached, when Mother came out of their bedroom in slippers and kimono.

'What do you think you're doing?'

Dad gave a sharp tug on the cord. The bonking increased rapidly, alarmingly, in volume, developing into more of a rumbling.

'Ought to get up there and oil that flange,' mumbled Dad.

Then it happened.

The staircase folded down abruptly, settling into its designed position, as the bottom step touched the floor. Dad nudged it into place, then looked up with amazement and sudden terror as an indefinite number of hard round slithering, slightly prolate spheroids, brown, shiny, gleaming softly in the bleak dawn light, tumbled out of the rectangular dark space revealed by the adjustment of the staircase. They flung themselves about in a series of crazy arcs and whirls, bouncing from side to side against walls and staircase-well, making a stuttering drum-like sequence of sounds that accelerated alarmingly in tempo and increased in volume as the deluge of balls mounted in pressure.

Dad never got more than a step or two up the staircase when he was overwhelmed and thrown backwards onto the floor of the hall. The sound his head made striking the floorboards could barely be heard in the chorus of rumblings and thumpings, but Mother detected it and turned to flee to the ground floor. She never had a chance; the flood of leather from the attic caught up to her and over-rode her as she hurried down the stairs. They found her there later, smeared marks of brown leather polish along the backs of her legs and between her shoulders.

It would be impossible to guess how long it took for the cascade of leather to vacate the isolated bungalow, located towards the crest of a long rise out of the valley in which the village nestled. Medical investigators who examined Mother afterwards estimated time of death as shortly after sunrise, a few moments after the fatal attack on Dad. The attacks must have lasted a considerable time. Death, far from instantaneous, was much more like a case of being repeatedly bounced at, very unusual in forensic record. The bodies showed many minor subcutaneous lesions, crushings and bruisings of tissue, none of them sufficient in itself to cause death, but cumulatively destructive. Neither slow nor instantaneous, recalling the ancient capital sentence of pressing to death.

Miraculously the kids escaped unharmed, barring the shock of unlooked-for parent loss. The house too went almost undamaged. The hardwood floors and staircase, Mother's pride, were scored and indented; the walls were smudged; even the ceilings were stained here and there in tones of milk chocolate or ox-blood. But all the children were conscious of between sound sleep and half-waking was a sound they'd never heard before and never heard again.

It had rained most of the night, leaving a heavy overcast at dawn, mist, light drizzle, hardly any breeze. The weather conditions seemed to thicken and soften sound, so that the kids weren't terrified by the assault. What they heard from under the covers was a long drum-roll, a ruffle of bass grumbling, indistinct and unthreatening. They never even got out of bed, and were found there, huddled together in drowsiness, by the relief squads that came up the hill afterwards. When they rose and went to the windows they were surprised by the sight of the front lawn and the shrubs.

The overnight rain had soaked the grass and made it all pungy and squashy, bright green mixed with freshly turned sludge. Everywhere were the marks of the invasion; the whole front lawn was pockmarked hideously with precise round traceries, indentations so distinct and accurately stamped out as though executed by some giant backhoe. They might have been the marks left by the passage of a fleet of colossal gumballs.

The pocks almost seemed to spell something, in a code or script that hovered on the edge of intelligibility without ever conveying a clear message. Later investigators found this disquieting. From the precise form and slight variations in depth of the roundels in the mud, a statistical pattern could be deduced, or inferred, that described the rhythms and distribution of the bounces. Plainly the swarm must have numbered in the thousands, perhaps in the ten thousands. The rapid drumfire of accent could not have been maintained by smaller numbers.

It was as though (this was a fearful conclusion) the aggregate of spheroids was controlled in and of itself, by a collective intelligence directing the movements of the whole, like the flight instincts of a flock of Canada geese. In the traces left behind there were hints of that pattern of bird behaviour which dictates the position of the leader in the flight and causes the strong individual leading flyer to fall back to the rear of the V from time to time, there to soar and rest, supported by aftercurrents created by the beat of many wings as the flock traverses different layers of the firmament, alternations of heat and cold.

There was an element, perhaps more than an element, of instinctual, maybe even intelligent organization in the periodicity of ball motion. It seemed possible to detect a kind of ebb and flow, or wavelength, in the marks stamped out in the damp mud and grass. But even the closest scrutiny proved incapable of reducing the copious supply of data to an order dictated by some hypothetical construct. Where did they come from? Where were they headed? Could they even be thought of as 'they', or should the flock or swarm be treated as an 'it', a single agency with conscious life and malign purpose? Was there something here of the structural nature of a bacterial culture? Perhaps, more menacing, there could be something of the symptomology of an unknown virus.

Whatever directed the movements of the flock or swarm, there remained no doubt about their positioning. There was a brief pause on the roadway in front of the house, as they took head and reassembled their numbers, in an apparently endless stream of reinforcement. Then they started down the slope towards the village, in form and motion something like a tornado or whirlwind, bowing and undulating in novel, terrifying movements. The sound they made seemed the worst element of their approach, because of its unfamiliarity and unlikeness to anything the villagers had heard before. Accounts of it after the fact are varied, but agree generally on the most impressive quality of the sound, depth, sonority, a deep bass-baritone humming tone, audible long before the flowing waving vortical aggregation became visible in the distance.

At 7:30 a.m., having recruited their numbers and formed up in some obscure pattern of migratory movement, the volleyballs moved to the crest of the long descent into the village. Intention of attack now took shape; the ground at the top of the hill shows the marks of thousands of arcs, spinning rotary etchings in the dirt, made by the hard firm over-inflated leather surfaces. Sometimes these motions dug into the cheap paving of the local highway, a feeder route for the throughway, in such a way as to throw up ridges of crumbled asphalt on either side of the cut. There was no effort at concealment.

Just before 8:00 they gathered themselves into a peaking, diving mass, alive with intersecting motions, and rolled forward and down the incline, gathering speed and agglomerating their mass into a clotted, murderous, serpentine array. Some of them may have bounced a hundred feet in the air as they passed. Evidence gathered from the torn bark of trees lining the route shows that oaks and maples a century old, some of them eighty feet tall, were bruised and crushed, their foliage ripped, branches cracked and split, by high-bounding projectiles. One weaker volleyball became lodged – so it seems – in a notch where a branch of an oak met its massive trunk.

There is some suggestion that a group of the balls came to their trapped associate's help, pounding strongly at the tree trunk so as to free up their companion and leave no straggler behind.

Can this be a sign of individual intelligence in these beings, or were they obeying primal group instinct? There is no way of knowing.

Halfway down the long slope, proceeding now at a thunderous pace, the swarm encountered a solitary old man moving slowly towards the hilltop, supporting himself by a simple walking-stick broken from the branches of a dead maple lower down. This poor man, half blind and more than half deaf, can never have understood the fate that now overtook him. He never tried to run, made no effort to turn aside or avoid contact. He was simply flattened, overrun, peppered with a thousand bounces and left for dead. The blind still face, examined afterwards by medical personnel, showed no emotion, or almost none. There was the look of somebody who had been tickled to death, but this may have been a misinterpretation.

Whatever the nature of the violence inflicted on the old man, there was no doubt in the minds of the villagers that something awful was about to come down on them. Brash teenagers who ventured towards the swirling curvetting mass suddenly became appalled at the pace and purpose of the dizzying motion, and turning began to scream and run away in every direction, crying: 'Run for your lives, the volleyballs are coming!' This dreadful warning brought the villagers to their doors, old women, nursing mothers, grandfathers, working men about to depart for their jobs. Their children frightened them with the terrible outcry; panic rose and spread. It was like a gospel warning. 'Woe unto them that are sick in those days or give suck at the breast.' The killer swarm came nearer and nearer and then debouched upon the village green, just where the roadway widened and circled the small sodded space that lay in front of the reeve's office and the sheriff's cantonment.

Fortunately for her, the reeve was away in the city that day, on some private business linked to the supply of a commodity that she distributes locally. The sheriff was less lucky. When they arrived in the village centre, the wilful uncaused dance of the balls increased in pace, showing no signs of ending. Witnesses later claimed that some individual balls rose more than twice the height of any village building including the church steeple, in their mad reboundings. There is evidence to suggest that the laws of dynamics were obeyed by the swarm. Their collective motion has been compared to that of a mass of corn in the popper, each individual kernel brought up to poppoint according to its own innocent necessity, but the whole troop showing obedience to statistical law, first one kernel going pop and then another, and then more, and more, in a percussive musical rhythm. The balls certainly behaved like corn in the popper, first one and then another and then whole clumps shooting into the air, impelled by powerful secret forces.

For some time it seemed as though this massive energy release might be the only show of strength exercised by the balls. The villagers began to peek out of doors and windows in the hope that the mysterious phenomenon was drawing to a close. But they were wrong. About 9:30, when the demonstration of leaps and bounces had risen to a frenzied state, the rhythm and motion began to change. They settled down into themselves and assumed once again the form of a waterspout or tornado in rapid forward motion. Their target was clear. The sheriff's cantonment lay directly in their path. Two of the fleet of squad cars that blocked them were lifted up and thrown across the village green to land crushed and flaming in front of the hardware store. The chain-link fencing surrounding the official building was abruptly breached; the volleyballs swarmed inside. There was a sound of shrieking and then a horrid quietness as the taut round leather objects assumed the form of a flying ribbon of silk and the sound of a swishing running caress. They flew out of the doors and windows in their thousands, regrouped themselves and dashed away down the narrow roadway towards the throughway clover leaf, just out of sight on the other side of low hills but always audible through the darkest night. The killer volleyballs had come and gone. The village folk stood around in stunned silence. Finally the deputy sheriff, braver than the others and schooled to risk, tiptoed into the sheriff's ruined quarters. Off balance on strained hinges, the door swung slowly shut behind him. The onlookers drew quiet frightened breath, waiting, waiting. The door creaked open. The ashy-faced deputy leaned out. He put a finger to his lips.

'Spiked!'

All they heard for the rest of the long day was the noise of crashings and bangings of multi-car pileups off in the distance, and the sound of windshields starring into powder.

Swedes in the Night

(For Frances Heinsheimer Wainwright)

Francesca had done a year *au pair* in Katrineholm near Stockholm, almost becoming a member of the Swedish host family in the course of the stay. She and Minna, the eldest Roelofsen daughter, had become like sisters; they arranged for Minna to visit her friend in Parma the following summer, bringing Francesca back with her to Sweden for a refresher visit, to see old friends and renew certain ties with the young men of the northern town. The young women met in Parma towards the end of June and spent an exciting ten days exploring the region. Like many young Europeans they used the railways as though they formed an enormous métro.

Minna was thrilled by her sight of the famous repositories of art and music: Bologna, Vicenza, Ravenna, Modena. Entry to the opera house of Modena especially excited her. It was there that the great Pavarotti had launched his career. The young women felt no fear of strangers during these frequent short journeys by rail. They felt that ordinary sensible conduct, avoidance of isolated platforms after dark, little use of over-the-shoulder bags, inconspicuous outerwear, allowed them to travel in perfect freedom over long distances without interference or unwelcome solicitations from strangers. It was decided towards the end of Minna's stay in Parma that they should return to Katrineholm together just after the beginning of July, making the journey by one of the north-south express services that bisect western Europe, not by TEE, the most costly Eurorail accommodation, but by the next most expensive service, rapid express, first class, departing from Milano at 22:35.

On the morning of their departure, Francesca's father drove the young women the short distance to the station. They were taking a leisurely ride into Milano by local, arriving early in the afternoon. They might do some recreational shopping, small gifts for the younger children, for the parents, for remembered boyfriends, afterwards dining near the station and boarding their train well in advance of departure so as to have a good choice of accommodation.

Naturally everything went as planned; these two shared some qualities of prudence, efficiency, solid good sense, that had helped to make them close friends in spite of their widely separate upbringing. An unusual aspect of their relationship was the fact that Francesca, like many women of northern Italy, was fair-headed and blue-eyed, while her friend was a brunette with dark-brown, almost black eyes. They sometimes joked about this, calling themselves the big Swede and *la bella ragazza* and defying acquaintances to determine which was which. Sometimes for a joke they would address themselves by each other's names. They got used to answering to either, so that Minna might reply to calls for 'Cesca at home or abroad, while her friend would equally respond to inquiries addressed to Miss Minna. They enjoyed this intimate tie.

A shortish visit to the Brera, then and for a long time afterwards in baffling *restauro,* and an enormous shared pizza which prepared them to do without nourishment until the next morning, left them with two or three hours on their hands before departure. The district around the central station in Milano has an unsavoury reputation. Watch out for bands of gypsy dancers! A common bit of travellers' lore. So Minna and 'Cesca located an empty bench across from the south entry to the enormous building, near the taxi ranks and the *gelata* wagons. At half-hour intervals airport buses arrived from Malpensa. A short, neatly dressed, very good-looking taxi driver hung around the signpost marking the taxi stand, casting admiring glances in their direction. Once he seemed to be on the point of crossing the little square and speaking to them, but the long Milanese twilight had by now begun to deepen, and he made no move. Minna and 'Cesca finished their orange drinks, shouldered rucksacks and moved into the station. It was now about 21:40; their train was almost ready for boarding. A smallish crowd had started to form at the gate; perhaps the train would not be very full tonight. In another few minutes the barrier was swung open and coincidentally a series of announcements in Italian, German, Flemish, English, Danish and Swedish made it clear that the express for the north was now receiving passengers and would depart on schedule. Travellers would kindly attend to the wording of the placards affixed to the several cars, checking their numbers against those given on their tickets. Through cars for the far north were located at the head of the train.

The route of this express varies from night to night; sometimes you go north on the right bank of the Rhine. At other times the train veers northwest, taking travellers through Stresa, Basel, Mulhouse, Strasbourg, then back into Germany through Mainz, Bonn, Hamburg, Lübeck and on into Copenhagen, thence forward by ferry into Sweden, continuing north to Göteborg and then northeastwards to Katrineholm (the girls' destination) and at last into Stockholm, a longish ride but an exciting one. Minna and 'Cesca had chosen this latter route.

Before boarding they equipped themselves with the ordinary rail travellers' supplies, slabs of dark chocolate, Agatha Christie paperbacks in Italian, several large bottles of *frizzante* to quench thirst during the ride. They were heavily slung about with bottles and carryalls depending from parts of their clothing as they moved along the platform towards the head of the train. As they neared the engine they passed a second-class carriage, brightly lit and partly filled with passengers coming and going in the corridor seeking the most favourable positions for rest, access to lavatories, a smooth ride; the girls might have been observed from this carriage. The adjacent car proved to be the first-class vehicle going all the way.

The young women noticed that there now seemed to be more travellers about than they'd observed at the gate. Maybe the train would be better than half full after all. They moved determinedly along the passageway, peeking in the windows of successive cubicles, wanting to start off in a compartment to themselves. If they were fortunate they might keep it private overnight. There would be a stop at Strasbourg about 6:35, when they would be able to purchase materials for breakfast. Passengers might then invade their stronghold, but they would have enjoyed a first night by themselves. Both veteran rail travellers, they stopped two-thirds of the way along towards the front of the car and darted sidewise into an empty cubicle which when full could accommodate eight first-class passengers. As they set their water bottles, chocolate slabs, rucksacks and other impedimenta down, they felt the car jerk forward, then back, then forward again, and the train moved slowly out of the station on its way to the north. It was exactly 22:35 and the twilight had deepened almost into night. They examined their temporary home together.

They were in a first-class day coach, not a *wagon-lit*. Facing each other across a roomy floor-space were two overstuffed bench seats upholstered in a noticeably convex, dusty cloth which exhaled sizeable motes of matter when one bounced or rolled on it. These long seats could be slid out from the wall by tugging at their frame, in such a fashion as to form a pair of couches. As many as four persons could lie side-by-side in the compartment, with a narrow space between couples. Intermittent slumber and restorative horizontal relaxation were thus sometimes obtainable. Francesca and Minna had hoped to find themselves in just such a car, so as to conserve the premium payment for overnight sleeper service. As the train proceeded towards the foothills, they tugged energetically at the two seats, arranging them as undraped couches. They didn't undress, merely put aside their outer jackets. In a few minutes they had arranged the compartment very conveniently, drawing the curtains across the sliding doors and the small windows that looked out on the passageway.

Towards midnight a senior train official passed along the corridor, paused, and tapped quietly at their door. He put his head in to see how they were getting along and nodded in a fatherly way at the sight of their cosy arrangements. If they wished, he indicated, he might find them a pair of blankets; this friendly offer was declined. The night was warm and the air-conditioning ineffective. They would just lie down fully dressed. When they awoke they would be in Strasbourg and ready for breakfast.

For another three-quarters of an hour they kept the lights on at their lowest setting, pinpricks of faint orange glow in near-darkness. Then in unspoken agreement they reached up and put their lights out. Each stretched out on one of the firm smelly seats, with the narrowed floor-space between; it was completely dark in their cubicle. They fitted themselves into and around the lumps and bumps and eventually dozed off.

This semi-improvised sleeping accommodation is never altogether satisfactory, as everybody who has tried it knows. Both girls woke from time to time, not simultaneously, as the train climbed into Switzerland and the mountains; awake or asleep they shared a sense of the sharp incline. Soon the night was half gone. The pair were sound asleep when the train stopped for several minutes at Basel. Perhaps they were partly aware in their sleep of the deep still-ness that had invaded their compartment; they murmured and rolled over. The train slid quietly out of Basel station and headed for Mul-house. Did it make another stop there? They were never sure after-wards. And they slept on.

This quiet overnight rest was shattered, blown away in seconds, sometime around 3:30, the hour when vitality burns lowest and inti-mations of mortality assail dreams. BOOM ... CRASH ... WHOOP ... THUMP ... BONK.

On came the lights at their fullest. Giant paws reached around the doorframe to activate the switches and roll back the sliding panels thunderously. There was a stupefying odour of alcohol, incom-pletely assimilated by the drinkers' metabolisms. Great noise, much factitious jollity. The two young women sat up suddenly, dazed by this invasion and half-blinded by the harsh glare. The data of three senses seemed to attack them: stench, dizzying light, deafening con-fusing sound. What was happening was phantasmagorical, impossi-ble to cope with adequately without notice.

Thank God they hadn't undressed! In unspoken agreement the girls sat straight up and began to mouth warnings and dismissals. As they rose to their feet they felt the car begin to sway slightly as the train accelerated on a flat stretch. It was completely dark outside. Where were they? Who were these awful people?

They were two enormous blond statuesque foul-smelling Swedish youths who had either boarded the train at its most recent stop, or somehow found their way into the first-class accommoda-tion from the adjoining coach, and they were overjoyed at these treasures, two nubile persons in a surprised, defensive, possibly per-suadable posture. These unlooked-for men plainly expected ecstatic accepting response, an illusion nicely proportioned to their degree of drunkenness. No hint of rejection could have made its appropri-ate impression on them, and the sources of intoxication were not far to seek. Each man carried a large bottle of what could only be, from its odour, the finest Hollands, a rich scent of juniper at once pervading the swaying space.

The intruders began to sing loudly, in the jolliest manner, reaching out for the girls with carefree gestures. Each had a single hand available at the end of a long arm, the other hand and arm cradling their bottles. As Francesca got stumblingly to her feet, staring at her would-be partner, she was reminded absurdly of young babies who balance themselves erect at about eleven months, nursing bottles suspended between hungry lips by the rubber nipple. The man she was staring at, his face forty centimetres from hers, had a mutinous pursy-lipped babyish grimace of desire on his features. A long forearm coiled towards her. Minna, meanwhile, had bent forward in the direction of the locomotive, leaning down to force the bench seat into its daytime position. This was an erroneous tactic; the drunk nearer her at once began to make wide, ill-directed swipes at her buttocks, doubtless intending awkward endearment.

Minna now spoke between clenched teeth. 'Get your seat back; we need room.' Her companion thereupon rocketed upwards, pushing from her heels until she stood fully erect. She was a tall girl, only slightly shorter than the male who confronted her. He reeled back and Francesca pushed hard with her calves against the seat which slid smartly back against the wall.

Now the struggle began in earnest. Adjustment of the seats had opened an oblong space for manoeuvre something like a small boxing-ring, and the tactics of the ensuing engagement much resembled those of a championship boxing match, or more closely still a tag-team wrestling encounter. The girls concentrated intensely on the proportions of the ring and the slow fuddled movements of their antagonists. There remained ninety minutes before dawn light, perhaps another two hundred and fifty kilometres before Strasbourg; they would have to fight a canny delaying action. Neither had the slightest wish to comply with the clear wishes of their intoxicated visitors.

The girls began to circle the compartment, moving in opposite directions to confuse pursuit. They exchanged tactical advice as they passed, never using their given names in the same way consecutively;

this confused the interlopers, who couldn't distinguish the big Swede from *la bella ragazza*. As Minna and 'Cesca bumped into one another in circling, they whispered words of encouragement, at the same time stifling laughter. There were frequent pauses in the struggle as the invasive males briefly lost control of their movements; these interruptions resembled the rests between rounds of the ordinary boxing match. All that seemed wanting was a referee, and of course a bell or gong.

The girls addressed no words to their hilarious visitors beyond an occasional 'Damn you, my stockings', or 'Filthy beast!' But there was a lot of noise generated during the engagement as first one male and then the other fell heavily against or on his quarry, pulling a girl down full-length on one of the bench seats. Then there were moments of silent struggle. Minna bit one of them on the lobe of his left ear, bringing much blood and many exotic curses. Kickings. Male implorings. At one point 'Cesca found herself lying full-length on top of her willing boyfriend, thrashing around and trying to break an embrace that appeared to be strengthening. A fugitive despairing impulse to relax and enjoy it sped through her mind, but that would be to betray herself and her friend, and she redoubled her struggles. How long till Strasbourg? How long had they been defending themselves? Would it never be day? It seemed so dark. She half stood up, and slapped vigorously at the babyish face, and then the sliding doors opened miraculously with their unmistakable rumble. The *chef de train* and five of his associates appeared clustered in the doorway.

Sizing up the situation at once, the *chef de train* yanked the communications cord and amazingly the train braked to a sudden halt, throwing everybody off balance. The two intoxicated Scandinavians fell heavily against the forward wall, stunning themselves. In this state they were bundled out of the compartment and along to the end of the car nearest the head of the train. It was still completely dark. As the girls peered out of their windows they realized that the train had stopped right on the main line in the middle of what seemed to be dense forest. The forms of their late assailants now flew gracefully out of the forward exit to land heavily and no doubt painfully on the ballast of the right of way, some little distance from the tracks. The train at once resumed its forward progress, quickly working up to full speed as the two Swedes got to their hands and knees, baggageless, a hundred kilometres from anywhere.

'And as far as I know they're still there,' says Francesca when she tells the story, laughing, thinking of her vanished youth.

Too Much Mozart

The distressing incidents of the closing weeks of 1991 have been the occasion of much curious but fruitless speculation among members of the concerned public, without any systematic inquiry's having yielded an account of these matters satisfying alike to the subtlety of the trained investigator and to the grosser perceptions of the mass of opinion.

It may be that enough time has now elapsed to allow of a more complete explanation of the circumstances leading up to the tragedy, the distant hidden causes, the more proximate provocations, the failure of local authority to identify potential disaster while it stared observers in the face, so as to dispel a cloud of rumours, half-truths, misdirected suspicions and conspiracy theories, and finally to give a clear, full and responsible description of the entire matter. Those of us who have been permitted access to all the dossiers annexed to the dreadful event now feel that the passing of a decade – the coming on of a new century, a new millennium, a more hopeful age – should permit frankness in the review of the affair. One hopes, naturally, to cause no traumatic rupture of the emotional scar tissue which may have formed over the memories of those whose dear ones suffered during that black night in East Sequoia, California.

The little 'town of the giant redwoods' lies in the north-central region of the Golden State, separated by a considerable distance from the arid wastes of the south, but adjacent to the fault line which may be connected to the state of febrile excitement characteristic of the citizenry of the place. It was here, in the almost subtropical climate of the district, that the administration of the state university chose in 1971 to erect a new campus devoted wholly to the study of music in all its aspects: composition, ear-training, performance, musicology, criticism. In the next two decades, East Sequoia became filled at all hours of the day and night with music of every kind, flowing from the studios of conservatories and rehearsal halls, and from the windows of passing automobiles, from the lips of casual whistlers along Sepulveda Boulevard. Arias floated from ranch-style motels where accommodation was available by the night or the week or the semester. Percussionists transported marimbas to the banks of the dry course of the North Sacramento River for working picnics. Music became inescapable.

It will be remembered that throughout the fateful year 1991, the bicentenary of the death of the composer W. A. Mozart had been commemorated by incessant, round-the-clock performances of his music, and his son's music and his father's music. Every last scrap which might be assigned, with the smallest reason, to the prodigious invention of the renowned Austrian, whether finished or unfinished, or of dubious provenance, fragmentary, or almost certainly the work of some anonymous *seguaci* of the celebrated artist, every morsel was to be unearthed, rehearsed, polished, played over and over again. This questionable undertaking issued in the performance of many pieces that had better been allowed to moulder in the archives of Lambach or Melk. Violin and keyboard sonatas of great insignificance, numbered K. 6, 7, 8, now saw the light of day for reasons having nothing to do with their musical merit.

Whether the cause of the composer was forwarded by this exposure to a mass of immature apprentice work must remain conjectural. It is, however, certain that the deluge of late eighteenth-century music that developed from the uncritical Mozartolatry of the day contributed materially to the chain of causes that led to the infamous mass slayings at the Burger Heaven outlet in East Sequoia.

A fashion or modish trend may sometimes cause immense harm by imposing itself upon masses of people who inwardly deeply disapprove of its tendency. Mozart is all very well in his way, but so is country and western, although its chords and melodies may seem to a refined musical taste remote from the more complex structures favoured by classical composers. An omnipresent Mozart or Tchaikovsky may insult the ears of captive listeners as much as acid-rock or rap. Certainly the townspeople of East Sequoia included many music students and professors and ordinary citizens who might prefer Mozart to Michael Jackson. But the reverse is equally true, and the bicentenary observations that continued throughout 1991 tended to overbalance the scale in favour of the Mozart-lover.

By the time ten months of the anniversary had gone by, East Sequoia was peopled quite largely by folks who privately or at large deplored the unending performance of the lesser productions of the infant Mozart, as an invasion of their right to enjoy the music of their choice.

Merle Huggins was night manager of the Calestoga Supermart in the centre of town on Sepulveda Boulevard. A quiet, almost withdrawn man of thirty-two, Merle rarely gave any indication of the stresses that must have fissured his personality. Married, childless, he lived with his wife Eleanor in a bungalow on South Sacramento Road, out where the trees and shrubs disappear and the water-supply problem shows itself.

He drove the mile and a half into town each evening in a late-model Chevy Celebrity, parking the vehicle in his reserved slot in the supermarket lot. Burger Heaven lay directly in line with his parking space. Sometimes Merle would drop into the restaurant for a quick coffee before going on shift. About 4:00 a.m. he would either send one of the bag boys for burgers and fries, or come over himself. Midweek he usually came in himself, to sit for an hour on his break, and consume the round-the-clock big breakfast: two eggs lightly over, German sausage, four strips bacon, slice of melon, home fries, wheat cakes and syrup, toast, marmalade and coffee. Energy food. He would listen to the piped-in music with close attention. The restaurant staff testified to his keen interest in folk and western, with some blue grass.

During the year-long bicentenary festivities, the local Muzak licensee tended to program more Mozart Muzak than usual. This wasn't quite so noticeable during the first quarter of 1991, when the most familiar of the composer's greatest hits were being played. Nobody in his right mind could reasonably object to the very frequent repetitions of the 'Eine Kleine Nachtmusik', K. 525, with which the patrons of Burger Heaven were now being favoured. And as the year drew on other less familiar masterworks from the Köchel catalogue were often to be heard, the lovely 'Serenade for Thirteen Wind Instruments', K. 361, for example. Similar masterpieces abound in the Mozart catalogue, and these were for some time the most often heard.

By about July, however, the incessant repetition of the composer's works brought broadcasters, recitalists, FM radio and the Muzak services close to the bottom of the barrel. Inferior Mozart now surfaced. Some of the public felt jaded, surfeited by this musical fare. The night staff of the Burger Heaven noted that Merle Huggins sometimes seemed moody and restive as the cascade of baroque, rococo and *galante* compositions continued to issue from the ceiling loudspeakers above the serving counters and the no-smoking section. Because of its central location Burger Heaven functions as a meeting place for students and instructors for the UCES facility situated a short distance away on the west side of town.

At any hour of the day or night musical practitioners, tubaists and typanists and mezzos and coloraturas and basses and all sorts of other musicians could be found seated in the no-smoking section of Burger Heaven, humming to themselves and pounding out sophisticated rhythms on the tabletops, sometimes bursting into full-scale performance, quartet, trio, passages for four voices from the *Litaniae Lauretanae*, K. 195, or some lesser choral work. An unprejudiced observer might have noticed tell-tale signs of rage and frustration on Merle Huggins's face, as the sacred strains wafted through Burger Heaven at 4:00 a.m. But in 1991 everybody was a Mozart fan, as decreed by the musical press and the FM broadcasters. A sadly amusing aspect of this situation, rarely noted during the festivities, was the fact that the composer's music lay in the public domain, copyright having long since expired. None of Mozart's descendants profited to the extent of one penny from the bicentenary performances. The exact location of Mozart's grave, a pauper's grave, remains questionable. It rained hard on the day of the composer's funeral; more than half of the eleven mourners in the procession turned back halfway to the cemetery.

Somehow this troublesome fact had lodged in Merle Huggins's mind. It seems to have obsessed him. He would mutter to himself over his hash-browns, during these impromptu Mozart tributes, phrases like 'dumb sons of bitches', and 'lots of thanks he ever got', and 'not a red cent'. He seems to have identified the dead Mozart's interests with his own.

A series of peculiar incidents involving Mr Huggins now took place. Long past midnight on a Monday night towards the end of October, two music students visited the Calestoga Supermart for dips and chips and six-packs. In the course of their visit they happened to pass the night manager as he moved along the party snacks aisle, checking the stock. One of the students dropped a casual remark attributing the authorship of the two doubtful 'Lambach' symphonies, K. 45a and 45b, to the young Mozart. All at once the two students heard a throaty growl, and turning around they saw Merle Huggins coming at them in a rage.

'He never wrote those pieces of shit,' shouted Huggins. 'Maybe Leopold wrote one of them. I'll give you that, but the other is crap right the way through.' A fistfight broke out between the night manager and the younger of the music students. Then wrestling one another to the floor, they rolled along the aisle towards the pet food, where they toppled a pyramid of economy-sized cartons of Purina Dog Chow. The police came, and the incident was hushed up.

'I don't know what came over the guy,' said the younger student, a flutist, as he dabbed at his bloody nose. 'He seems to have this Mozart thing.'

A week after the incident, Merle Huggins was sighted in the gun boutique on Sepulveda, buying a bulletproof vest, the top-of-the-line model giving maximum protection to torso, neck and upper arms. He told the owner of the shop that he intended to go hunting and was afraid of being mistaken for large game while concealed in brush. No licence is required for such a purchase, and no record of it was kept. Mr Huggins brought his vest home and tried it on in front of the bureau mirror in his bedroom. His wife Eleanor noticed this but thought nothing of it.

Nor did she pay a whole lot of attention when Merle took off for a week in November without telling her where he was going. When he came home she figured that he'd been cruising the Bay Area, because he brought back a semi-automatic Heinsleben L-14, which is a popular hand weapon in San Francisco for defence against armed robbery, break-ins, street violence. After all, as Mrs Huggins said later, her husband worked nights and had a perfect right to protect himself against the waves of violence that sometimes rolled down from the north.

Merle himself made no attempt to conceal his possession of the gun. 'Right of every American to take up arms in his or her own defence,' he told Eleanor. 'There wouldn't be nearly so much of this date rape if a woman had the baldheaded goddam good sense to protect herself.'

'You couldn't take that thing on a date,' said Ellie, fondling the gun and sliding the bolt-action in and out. She liked the unmistakable metallic series of clicking noises that the firearm produced when being readied for action. 'Where's the safety?' she asked him.

'Right up here next to the trigger guard. And you can reset the weapon for fully automatic feed, just by sliding out this little catch.' He struggled with the device for some seconds.

'Here, clumsy, let me try,' said Eleanor. The superfluous part came away smoothly in her hands. 'Well, I never,' she said.

'Twenty-four rounds to a clip, and all you have to do is bump the trigger down and you get fully automatic fire. You can sort of spray it around and hose them down.' Merle showed her his supply of the heavy ammo slips, each holding two dozen rounds. 'Reloads almost instantaneously,' he said with satisfaction. 'You could hold off an army with this, if you had the guts, and a favourable defensive perimeter.'

For at least another week Merle seemed calmer and happier after this purchase. Then his Mozart problem resurfaced. On the following Sunday morning he came home from work, looking pale and drawn. Sunday night was his night off. He always went to bed very early to catch up on sleep arrears, but he didn't seem able to achieve refreshing oblivion. Next morning he reported a terrifying nightmare to his wife.

'I was tied to a kitchen chair and no matter how hard I struggled I couldn't free myself. They forced me to sit through all eight movements of the "Hafner Serenade", K. 250.' Ellie didn't know what to say to him; she reckoned that he'd regain his balance once Mozart Year was over. But then, in the second week of December, the students in the performance classes at the State U. announced a presentation of Handel's *Messiah* in the re-scored version by Mozart, sung in German. This desecration of the great Saxon's masterwork troubled Merle Huggins very deeply indeed. It was almost as though he had moved on to identify himself with Handel, violently rejecting any meddling with his sacred music drama.

The *East Sequoia Times* was filled with coverage of the upcoming oratorio, making much of Mozart's revisions, as though they amounted to a complete rethinking and updating of *Messiah*. On the night of the dress rehearsal Merle seemed almost distracted. He did something he almost never did. He came home around 2:00 a.m. for his break. He dressed himself in his bulletproof vest, checking the pockets for easy access to reserve ammunition. Half afraid, Ellie asked him where he was going.

'Going to get me some Mozart lovers,' said Merle.

'Naturally I thought he was only kidding,' said his wife later.

He wasn't kidding. He burst into Burger Heaven at 3:17 a.m. and slew twenty-three, wounding an additional nine including the night manager of the fast-food outlet, who couldn't understand Merle's actions at all.

'I thought we were really pals,' he said.

The state police SWAT team was quick to respond to the emergency call, and their remedial counter measures swiftly eliminated the problem. The lone killer was wounded in eight places, in the head, in the neck and lower limbs. Identification was easy even though the head was badly disfigured, the killer being a known and respected local man. One of the state police officers, kneeling beside the dying man, tried to question him about the causes of the slayings.

'Could you try to tell us why you did it, Merle?'

'Too much Mozart,' said Mr Huggins, as he closed his eyes.

The Bug in the Mug

(For Kevin Noordberg)

I don't think anybody would describe me as a neurotic woman sub-ject to compulsion without appeal, but I do like to find things where I left them. 'A place for everything and everything in its place' is the kind of maxim that leads to self-destruction if too rigidly insisted on; all the same it is the homemaker's bulwark against utter confusion. I keep cleaning materials under the sink, J-cloths, Mr. Clean, sos pads, but not Drano, which goes high up on a shelf, out of the reach of toddlers. There haven't been any toddlers around our house for fifteen years, but you do see what I mean. It isn't paranoia that ban-ishes Drano to a distant elevated corner, it's common sense. Or is it the onset of dreadful disturbance disguised as prudence?

I like to find things where they belong, never mind the deep form of behaviour that's implied. I came in from the cottage two nights ago to do some dusting and go over the mail. When I got in after a longish drive I was ready to enjoy a coffee and an hour in front of the box. But my mug was gone!

Every woman has a right to her own coffee mug. The National Action Committee on the Status of Women has decreed this to be a fundamental female right. We now have T-shirts with 'Don't mess with my mug' on them. There are fourteen mugs on hooks under the kitchen cabinets, enough for anybody to have a mug of his or her choice; why should anybody make off with mine? It isn't on one of the hooks; it sits on the counter between the pile of paper napkins and the currently opened package of English muffins. I got it on a premium offer from Melitta with a package of filters and a plastic filter-holder. It's a sweet mug, a little larger than some of the others and an elegant colour, pale eggshell with a clear glaze, almost a Chi-nese quality to the surface. Where's my mug, I thought.

What housewife, if she loseth a groat, doth not light her lamp and sweep diligently until she find it? Good question, I thought. Hah, it must be in the dishwasher! I yanked the door open and there were four bread-and-butter plates, two ordinary mugs and some tumblers, and a few cutlery items, neatly racked up but not washed; there was a faint smell of stale butter but not my mug. But of course it wouldn't be there. Just before leaving I'd had coffee in my recliner in the rec room in front of the TV. When I do that I sometimes forget to bring my mug upstairs. I've failed to collect it for as long as two or three days but very seldom for ten. I thought, poor little muggie, I'm coming to get you. Mummy make all nice and clean!

People tell me that primitive animism, which is apparently what I suffer from, is less and less found among our contemporaries. We shouldn't think of all our treasured little possessions as animals, conscious, smaller and more cuddly than ourselves, but I can't resist it. I always say goodbye, little cottage, or sometimes even Camp Cozy Cot, when I leave for the city, especially in September. I'll be back, little cottage, I'll see you next spring, I say to it. It's the same with mugs; they don't live forever but we treasure them while they're in the house, something like children. I went down to the rec room and sank back in my recliner and my fingers sought the handle of the mug just where it would be, but it wasn't there. I had expected that it would be ringed with brown and in need of a good scrubbing but I hadn't imagined that it would not be there. I strode around the basement in a tantrum and then I realized that it wouldn't do a bit of good. Somewhere in the universe was my missing mug or the broken bits of it. The poor little handle, broken off and all alone, like Van Gogh's ear. We know that nothing disappears from the sum total of reality; it has to be somewhere, downstairs, upstairs or in the garbage. I rushed back to the kitchen and turned out the most recent garbage onto the floor. Coffee grounds, the Saturday *Gazette*, a huge browned lump of soggy newsprint, some unidentifiable skeletal remains, perhaps the tag-ends of a bucket of chicken, two opened cans with their lids folded back dangerously. No shards, slivers, fragments.

It's easy to tell the difference between guilt and guilt-feelings. Nobody needs to feel guilty about having guilt-feelings because chances are you haven't done what you feel guilty about. But if you find your hands dripping with human blood, that's different. What's troubling you is probably guilt, not guilt-feelings. It's the same with anxiety. I'm not prone to anxiety-feelings but faced with a missing mug I'm legitimately anxious, quite a different experience. The only thing to do was to get onto our house-sitter, Wally, my son's roommate. It was past nine now, and dark, but not too late to phone the boys, who never seem to go to bed at all. I can call them at any time up to two in the morning and find them bright and responsive and ready to talk, with the TV vocalizing in the background. I got Wally at once.

'Wally, Wally, where's my mug?' I wailed. It sounded like the opening bars of a repulsive folk song. I changed my tone slightly and repeated, 'Wally, where's my mug?' I heard a gasp and a sudden intake of breath. He must have turned his face away from the phone. 'Frank,' he said, 'wouldn't you know? That was your Mum's mug.' I was bubbling with indignation. Smashed? Lost? Taken over to their apartment to eke out their scanty supply of dishes? The idea!

'I'd never have touched it if I'd known,' he said, coming back on the line. He sounded bewildered and fearful. 'It all happened so suddenly, and Frank wasn't in the house with me. I came over alone, to water the plants and air out the bedrooms. I was in the house for two hours. You know we try to check everything very carefully. I found some dust-mice upstairs and chucked them out. Some of them were really dust-rats. It's funny how that stuff clots up under the beds. I don't know where it comes from.'

'It's mostly car-exhaust from the street,' I said. I'm a careful duster and a leading dust-analyst. What we get on our street is a sticky deposit that comes off black on paper towelling. Not a healthy grey dust that rises up and floats in beams of sunlight but a filthy poisonous urban deposit that never stops coming, a bit like sin. 'I know you're good about dusting,' I said, 'it's an unwinnable war but it's important to continue the struggle. But we needn't resort to extreme measures like making away with our women's mugs.'

'I just grabbed the first one I saw,' he babbled. 'There must be a dozen of them along under the cabinets there and one was sitting on the counter right to hand, not on a hook, I mean. You know me, if I'd tried to free up one of the ones on hooks I'd have had them all rolling around on the counter or maybe the floor.'

This is true. Wally is straight as a die, but a clumsy boy.

'I cupped it,' he said.

'Cupped what?'

'The enormous bug.'

When he said this I took the phone from my ear and shook my head to clear it. 'What?'

'The enormous bug.'

I expected to see the enormous bug standing beside me flapping its wings or antennae or mandibles. What are mandibles anyway? Jaws? I'm not crazy about the idea of enormous bugs with mandibles.

'I turned it upside down over the huge bug in the sink,' he said. 'I'd just finished doing out the parrot cages and cutting fresh newspaper for the cage bottoms. My hands were covered with newspaper ink so I turned to the sink to rinse them off, and that's when I saw it. At first I thought it was a hallucination, a confused visual memory of one of the parrots, imprinted on the retina of some monstrous neural error.'

Wally reads a lot and picks up some strange phrases.

'Monstrous neural error?'

'That's what I thought but it wasn't a hallucination; it was one-hundred-percent real, an enormous winged creature crouching in the sink stopper, if you follow me. You know how the sink stoppers are made of perforated metal, to let water out and trap solids that you don't want going down the drain. They're a couple of inches deep, plenty of room for a big bug to snuggle down in. I don't know where it came from. One minute the kitchen was empty and kind of shadowy because I hadn't turned the strip lighting on. And the next minute there was this apparition in the sink. I couldn't tell how big it was because it had folded itself down into the sink stopper. It was moving its wings slowly and they were getting wet from the tap. My first impulse was to pick it up by a wingtip, but then I reconsidered. It might get away or sting me. Judging from the size of its body it must have had a wingspread of five or six inches. Kind of a shiny purplish-black with blotches of some pale colour on the wings, like a damned soul. So ... well, I cupped it. I reached over and grabbed the nearest mug and tipped it upside down over the bug. The wingtips stuck out on either side. I went and got a square of cardboard out of the pile of paper napkins on the counter. Then I rocked the mug gently and slid the cardboard under it, capturing the bug in the mug. I tried not to crush it or break the wings. We never know the quality of pain these creatures may feel. I wouldn't want my wingtips crushed. I lifted the whole arrangement out of the sink and held it to my ear. I had an impression that the bug might speak to me. It was some sort of large moth, I believe, or death-watch beetle. I could hear noises from inside the mug, soft silky sounds, flutterings, but no outcry. I think I'd have lost hold of the whole bag of tricks if that bug had said something. I was eager to get rid of it but I couldn't see myself crushing it or swatting it. A housefly, that's something else; they're not very clean and they transmit disease. But a thing six inches across cutting the airy way might be an immense world of delights closed to your senses five!'

'Come again?'

'We don't know what a big bug may experience,' he said morosely. 'I felt that I had to get it out of the house. I carried the mug down the stairs and out the side door onto the driveway. I had trouble opening the inner door and then the screen door but I managed it. Then I went along to the back of the driveway, under the lilacs. I left the mug standing upside down in a depression in the tarred surface just this side of the gateway to the garden, and unless your neighbours have knocked it over with their car it's still there. I'm sorry I haven't had the chance to retrieve it; the incident went right out of my mind.'

Repression, I thought, an open-and-shut case. I didn't rebuke Wally or threaten him with revenge or ban him from the house, but I did let him see that I was disquieted and upset; there's never any point in disguising your reactions, better to let the hurt and the disappointment show. So while I wasn't severe with Wally I was cool, even distant.

He apologized for another few minutes and then we hung up. This left me with the usual woman's errand of cleaning up some man's mess. I found the flashlight, magnetized to the refrigerator door, and checked it to make sure it was fully functional. I didn't want to be caught down the driveway in the dark. Then I tiptoed down the stairs to the side door and out into the night. There was a gentle breeze blowing, just strong enough to make a rushing sound in the cedars and lilac bushes. I flashed the light down the driveway and spotted the mug under the bushes, just at the side of the driveway. I switched the light off. In the dark, as my eyes grew accustomed to the night, it was easy to pick out the greyish cylindrical shape. I crept up to it and when I was beside it I peered down. I didn't use my flashlight because I didn't want to startle the bug if it was still living. I bent over and stared hard at the rim on the cardboard. There certainly seemed to be a pair of wingtips visible on either side of the rim. I listened as hard as I could. Was there a repeated soft flipping sound? Was the thing in the mug still alive? It was almost still in the dark; there was now only the softest whisper of air and a quiet rustling of leaves. Were those wings moving by themselves?

I'm not a naturally brave person. It took all the courage I could muster to lean over and work my palm under the damp imprisoning square of cardboard. I thought I might get bitten. Who knows what infections such a bite might cause? Suddenly I snatched up the mug, the contents and the cardboard, and scuttled back up the driveway and into the kitchen. It took plenty out of me. I leaned against the counter, set the things down on it, and sat down to catch my breath, quivering in every muscle and nerve.

But it had to be done. I'd never get to sleep if I didn't empty the mug and wash it out in the dishwasher at the hottest possible setting. I armed myself with a big dish-towel, ready to smother anything that might come at me, and then I turned my mug right side up. There lay the creature, exposed on the cardboard, dead, one of its wings split, teetering from side to side in some slight draught. I don't think it could have weighed an ounce, although it was a clear six inches across the beautiful purplish-black wings. The pale splotches on each wing were a deep peachy colour I'd never seen before. The dead thing was unexpectedly lovely. I blew on it gently and it almost seemed about to rise into the air. But it was dead.

I knew just what to do. I pinned the wings out at their full stretch and the next day I mounted it in an old cigar box, pressing it out flat in a bed of wadded Kleenex. I had a piece of glass specially cut to fit the box and I taped it into place, pressing the bug evenly into the

Kleenex so that it wasn't crushed or broken. Then I hung the mount on the rec room wall where I can admire it, about a foot above eye-level. What would it be like to be such a creature? Who knows what bugs suffer?

I found that my mug was deeply stained by some tobacco-coloured pigment, either strong coffee or some exudation from the body of the struggling insect, who can tell? I've washed it and washed it but I can't get the stain out. Who can drink from that cup?

Life in Venice

Brenda and Alfie love the place, especially Brenda, but they can't afford to live there, or so this year's guidebooks say. And yet by the exercise of low cunning and self-denial they've managed to spend quite a lot of vacation time in Venice, weeks and months of it if you reckon up the total of a dozen seasons. Their basic maxim is simple: 'Stay away from S. Marco and the Doge's Palace and don't buy anything you don't immediately need.' Glass and crystal, antique dolls' dresses, suede passport cases, miniature carnival masks, none of these qualify as immediate needs. An immediate need is the sort of article indigenous Venetians use themselves, when they need to write letters, or mollify a nasty flu-like chest and head cold.

Guidebooks and phrase books seldom deal with these wants. Alfie, disturbingly healthy, obviously slated for a long, contented middle age, is nevertheless prone to sinus colds or something damned like them, that keep him awake in the small hours. As soon as he lies down the tickle starts in his throat, and then the coughing. He sits up and props his back against the headboard and tries to fall asleep in this position, trusting that he will simply slump down on Brenda's side of the bed instead of falling the other way and ending up on the floor. 'Hate to trouble you, darling. Go back to sleep.'

'I can't understand a word you're saying.' (It's about two-thirty in the morning.) 'What have you done to your nose?'

'It's somethig from the canals, I don't thig it's catchig.' Two or three nights of this lead to concerted action. Search for a drugstore (*una farmacia*) nearby. Round behind the open-air vendors' booths by the Piazzale Roma? No luck. Plenty of souvenir stalls and places to buy ice-cream, but what's wanted is a real drugstore serving Venetians who have stuffed-up noses and tickles in the back of the throat. *Per il trattamento sintomatico delle affezioni delle prime vie respiratorie, accompagnate da tosse e catarro.* Not the kind of language you find in Berlitz, but when noted on the label of a little blue jar with a green plastic screw-on top it makes perfect sense. For symptomatic

treatment of affections (disorders? ailments?) of the primary repira-
tory tracts (why plural?) accompanied by coughing and catarrh.
Sure. *Tosse e catarro.* But you've trouble finding *una farmacia* and
then you've got to figure out a descriptive phrase or name for the
soothing product in the little blue jar.

Brenda and Alfie live at the Hotel Airone, have done so since the
first time they came to Venice, oh, it must be fifteen years ago. They
squeeze out successive visits by coming in the various off-seasons.
The last week of November and the first ten days of December are
favourites. Or sometimes around the feast of S. Marco, April 25th.
The water doesn't smell too high then and there aren't many people
around. They travel light. Brenda can cram an amazing amount of
stuff into a single stout carry-all, and Alfie just wears his socks for
two days instead of one, before changing.

But the Hotel Airone isn't exactly in the heart of the pharmacy district, and the Lista di Spagna is not the place to go looking for a drugstore, too many touristic menus to examine. Finally a kindly native
informs them of the location of the drugstore in the Campo di S. Giacomo dell'Orio, and off they go, past S. Simeone Grande (much
smaller than S. Simeone Piccolo, why?), heading always in an easterly
direction until they debouch in one of the most charming living
spaces in the world, wrapped around the church of S. Giacomo
which was already being *rebuilt* in the year 1225. The drugstore will be
found in the upper corner of the *campo* just as you take a right along a
narrow, much-trafficked *calle,* heading towards the fish market.

The *farmacia* has a plate-glass display window, exactly like a similar shop in any city in the English-speaking world, with all the usual
drugstore paraphernalia arrayed in neat pyramids and stacks. *Mister
Baby: Linea dermonutritiva sapone neutro. Gamma: Linea/oro di fazzo-
letti 4 veli.* Shampoos. Bathing caps. A tower built of little green
boxes with blue trim, bearing the legend *Pomata balsamica: uso
esterno.* At the top of this column of little boxes stands a small jar
bearing the elegant triangular logo enclosing the simple announce-
ment: VICKS.

And below that in red: VapoRub.

'*Posso avvere un''* (jar, what's jar?), '*un' bottiglia ... un vasetto piccolo
di VapoRub, per favore?*'

Smiles. A small sum in lire changes hands. Brisk walk back to the Hotel Airone, clutching small package. Think of buying chest-rub in your third language! Another blow struck for one's personal multi-culturalism. Alfie smiles proudly at Brenda as they turn in the hotel doorway and ascend the stairs. The proprietor, used to seeing them retire to their room in mid-afternoon, ignores the groans and sighs that now emanate from room 14, where Brenda is giving Alfie a neck and back rub.

'Pomata balsamica is onguent vaporisant in French,' murmurs Brenda luxuriously, as she slides glistening odoriferous palms around the base of Alfie's neck. Ten minutes of this will put him to sleep, she calculates. He needs his rest after last night's broken slumber.

'Vaporizing ointment,' he now remarks drowsily. 'Trilingual,' whispers Brenda. Aren't we civilized, they think, staying in a small hotel, counting pennies. Several generations of fiction about English-speakers resident in Italy recall themselves. Hawthorne, James, Morgan Forster, Simon Raven. The back rub issues in embraces and kisses blended with the heady scent of balsamic unguent.

In this way their latest springtime Venetian sojourn unfurls to their radical satisfaction. Fruit is cheap. Bel Paese can be found everywhere and peeling off the foil is one of the minor but genuine lunchtime pleasures. Fizzy water. Carrots carefully washed and scraped, crispy and so good for one's dentition. Next day, Alfie feeling much restored after a night of uninterrupted slumber, they assemble the materials for a satisfactory lunch on the spread of their roomy double bed. Prosciutto, cheese, *panini,* apples, carrots. Now Brenda produces their carrot-scraper from the recesses of the carry-all. It is a Canadian-made instrument some years old, shaped something like a stiletto, with a metal handle and a protruding parallel pair of dull blades that you draw along the carrot, shaving it clumsily and perhaps wastefully. Alfie watches as Brenda struggles with the ineffective instrument, which snags awkwardly in the firm carrot flesh.

'Tell you what, let's put the carrots aside – we can have them tomorrow or for a bedtime snack – finish up the rest of lunch, and go buy a new scraper. I'll treat you to a new one; it's getting close to your birthday.'

'But what is the word for carrot-scraper?' Hasty consultation of phrase books and Italian/English dictionary without result. There is no Italian expression for carrot-scraper, and yet Italians, and more particularly Venetians, must scrape carrots (does that sound obscene?). They certainly don't chew them with the good soil of the fields still clinging to the roseate surface.

'We'll think about it as we go. Maybe the desk clerk will know.' (He doesn't.) They finish their lunch, bundle the unscraped carrots in plastic wrap, and quit the hotel, bound down the *fondamenta di tre ponti* in the general direction of the Rio di S. Margherita where, Brenda is certain, they once passed a hardware store or smallwares boutique that had a pile of many kitchen implements in its window. Paring knives, corkscrews, bread knives, spatulas. That's where they'll locate a carrot-scraper but then, what to ask for? And is a hardware store really a *ferrovia*? (It isn't quite; the English term *ironmongers* gives us a clue.)

'I think *ferrovia* has something to do with the railway.'

'Well, exactly. *Ferrovia statale*, on all the railway cars; we should have realized. But it's something like that.'

'*Ferramenta?*'

'I think you've got it, and we'll know it when we see it.'

But they don't see the shop just at first, because in five minutes they get sidetracked down the Rio di S. Sebastiano towards the Zattere, and they are lost.

Not lost in the sense of not knowing where they are, lost in the sense of being unable to refrain from wandering away to the three churches that are the glory of the quarter. S. Sebastiano, Arcangelo Raffaele, and most charming of the trio, the tiny church of S. Nicolo *dei mendicoli,* hidden in the southwest corner of the Dorsiduro and never mentioned in popular press accounts of Venetian goings-on. Weird, shadowy, barbaric, gleaming, very small, the interior of S. Nicolo is a unique work of restoration, carried out by the British 'Venice in Peril' fund, and more noteworthy than any of a hundred celebrated church interiors in Venice or elsewhere.

This triangulation of places of worship invariably draws Brenda and Alfie out of the beaten path of Venetian perambulators. Instead of carrot-scraper search they spend two hours of the early afternoon moving slowly from the interior of S. Sebastiano, richly decorated by Veronese, who is buried there, through that of the Archangel Raffaele, radiant with the work of the Guardi (uncle? nephew?) And then on to S. Nicolo. Why *mendicoli?* Something to do with beggars, mendicants? Brenda and Alfie have never found anybody who knows or talks about the little church hidden in the serene backwater of the celebrated world.

Around 3:45 they stumble back into daylight from the entrancing half-light of S. Nicolo, their imaginations full of shadows and surprising recesses, and now they are ten minutes from their hotel; they've used up most of the afternoon … *there it is!*

'*La ferramenta!*'

Brenda is perfectly right. Dead ahead of them on the north side of the Rio di S. Nicolo, there's a small shop-front whose window had been shaded and whose door had been shut tight in the midday siesta when they'd been earlier. Now the door is open, the window uncurtained, and there in the window lies a jumbled heap of small tools and kitchen equipment. Sink-stopper. They don't even know the French name for sink-stopper. Strainers, and sieves for rinsing veggies. Pepper grinders. All these handy implements betray the unmistakable Italian aptitude for design. Efficient can-openers. Super-star lemon-crushers oozing kitchen chic.

'*Eccolà!*' exclaims Brenda joyfully, and they approach the door of the hardware (smallwares, notions?) shop almost at a run. The interior is shady and constricted, hung with larger items like saws and ball-peen hammers and hanks of copper wire. Brenda is sure that she has spotted some items from the Stanley line of tools, rasps and spokeshaves. Now for the crunch! They have to voice their need to the lean, gentlemanly, almost bashful vendor, without doubt the proprietor, who emerges from the back room to attend to their request. Here incomprehension supervenes. He evidently knows no English, and surprisingly no French. And they don't know what carrot-scraper is in French anyway. It must be some truly terrifying polysyllable in German, and in the complex Venetian argot it likely bears no resemblance to the standard Italian term, which in any case they can't recall. Perhaps they've never seen it written or heard it spoken. Life in Venice is full of charming pitfalls.

Broken Italian achieves nothing except the partial pacification of the shopkeeper, who plainly realizes that this isn't a holdup attempt. He smiles with great charm and asks, '*Inglese?*'

'*Canadese!*' they exclaim proudly.

Friendliness washes miraculously across this cagey Venetian face. '*Ah, si, si,* Toronto. Eastern Avenue. Centre Island!'

This astonishes them and they resort to mime. Alfie hates mime theatre and clown humour and will not play charades or indeed any game involving imaginative acting-out. Here, however, some non-verbal means of communication must be invoked, always a risky business given that body language varies remarkably from place to place. What you or I might act out to mime carrot-scraping could very well be misinterpreted by a Latvian, say, or an Albanian. The Venetian hardware man can make nothing of their improvised semiotic devices. Are they perhaps demented? Are they teasing him?

Brenda starts to breathe hard through her mouth as she tries to mime essential carrotness.

The hardware man leans forward, his face contorted in his effort to understand. All at once she remembers her notebook, takes it out, tears a sheet of paper and motions a request for a writing implement which he supplies, a felt-tipped pen certainly taken from stock. She seizes it and draws what she considers to be the unmistakable outline of a swelling carrot. The man examines it. His face colours. He begins to wave his arms. He is embarrassed and perhaps angry. On a second look Brenda recognizes that her rendering of a carrot is widely open to misunderstanding, and she blushes in her turn. The proprietor is about to retreat into the back room when Alfie saves the situation.

'*No no no, non ha capisce.*' (He isn't sure what this means.) Inspiration strikes from nowhere. '*Una cosa per grattare la carote.*' Brenda stares at him with gratifying wonder and admiration. The hardware store man, suffused with human understanding, smiles, bows to Brenda as if to apologize for unbecoming suspicion, and goes to the display window, from which he recovers precisely what they were looking for, the newest, best-designed Italian model of carrot-scraper. Unlike your ordinary Canadian article it is built to last, from some light, softly shining, stainless alloy curved in a delicate but strong horseshoe shape, with the open end of the shoe crossed by the doubled cutting blade, which is set at the most efficient angle imaginable.

The thing is a miracle of the principles of engineering, and sub-industrial design, as applied to ordinary human need. It is the best-designed and longest-wearing and most efficient carrot-scraper in the world.

Brenda affirms this for years after its discovery on the sunlit afternoon Venetian street. It has lasted for twenty years and isn't worn out yet, and every time one of them cleans a carrot, bright orange topped with green contrasting with the soft metallic sheen of the scraper, he or she recalls the three churches of the quarter, the glamorous works of Veronese, the altarpieces of the Guardi, the mysterious interior of S. Nicolo *dei mendicoli* swimming in candlelight, shadowy figure of the Blessed Virgin Mary slowly coming towards you in the dim light, wrapped in an old red velvet evening dress.

Plumbers

It's late afternoon – the most tension-relaxing time of the day – and Bronson is in the tub, the door to the bathroom about halfway open so as to keep the space warm and not too steamy. The tub is long and wide and he can float in it, his back just barely touching bottom. Vapour rises from the gently rippling water. He can almost, not quite, stretch his legs out full. He is turning a soft pink. He plays his usual bathtub games. Chases a small ball of wet wool around the side of the tub; each time he tries to capture it the tiny black object floats out of his clutch. The thing is to form a cup of your palm, slide it under the wool, lift hand gently, don't make waves, easy now … there! No, it got away. It takes five tries but he finally traps it, uncups his palm and identifies it as a bit of material from the socks he was wearing, probably trapped between his toes before he immersed himself. Any other bobbing objects? No, but there goes the soap, oops. It doesn't float. Now it's gone down somewhere under his thighs; he can't see it; it's around behind him; now it's swirling down to the other end of the tub, the primrose-coloured form just visible six inches below the surface. Water starts to slop over. He seizes the soap and deposits it in the aperture in the wall for safety. Pauses to admire the design of this little recess; the bathroom is fitted out with 1930s elegance, the tile is a gorgeous apple green.

The soap safely stowed, he leans back full-length and arranges his washcloth in an oblong on the surface. He can smooth it flat and it seems as though it will float. This is his favourite tub game, seeing how long his washcloth will float. Eventually it begins to sag slightly, losing its geometrical definition and starting to look like some submarine sea-beast, perhaps a giant ray.

Dimples and little valleys appear in the richly flocked pale peach cloth. Its edges begin to assume lovely serpentine forms. The whole swatch of material sinks … sinks … and wraps itself sculpturally over Bronson's genitals, outlining them in high relief in a hue resembling that of the peach-coloured marble used in some Roman church interiors of the Renaissance.

He rearranges the washcloth on the surface. This time it sinks onto his lower belly and plasters itself deeply into his navel.

Now he extends his right leg as far as he can and arches the big toe up and away from the other toes, pulling it upwards and back towards him so as to insert it with surgical exactness into the single tap at the other end, which is just big enough to accept this invasive gesture. He retracts the toe and there is a faint but perfectly audible popping noise, like that made when you snap your forefinger out of your tensed cheek and lips to amuse a baby. He reinserts the toe in the tap and is keenly pleased to note that he can sense, through the fresh plump flesh, the presence of a rim or groove just inside the mouth of the tap. He is able to rotate the big toe – it must be the right toe – slowly so as to feel a grinding action between the toe and metal rim. It is a pleasure obtainable, he thinks, in no other way.

This perception seems to him to strike at the roots of metaphor.

He worries the reflection briefly – he is in sales and marketing – and then drowses, half-aware of the nice letter he got this morning from Jolene and Bubba who are administering the Beiderbecke festival in Davenport, Iowa, hears footsteps on the stairs and gets the big toe out of the tap. Could this amusement be ranked as a solitary vice? The footsteps accelerate and the bathroom door flies fully open, a wavelet of coolness swinging through the doorway. He shrinks back into the warm water until only his face is above the surface, his ears submerged. Viv looms in the doorway, arms akimbo. Akimbo, he thinks, fine word, never heard in spoken English. Where from? Old Norse *kene bowe*. He can't hear what she is saying because the bath water has stoppered up his ears. Rises to the surface like a victorious U-boat in a World War II film.

And Viv repeats, 'We've got a problem.'

* * *

Now we flash back a couple of weeks, to the point where it became evident that the bathroom basin wasn't draining properly. Sluggish rotation of water, back-feed of hair and questionable grey solid particles, greasy feel of drain when finger used to probe. Slow access of homeowner's angst. Why does the tub drain all right while the basin is almost blocked? Is there something in the U-trap? Is the blockage lower down? What are those prolonged glug-glug, gurgle-gurgle sounds emitted by the plumbing when both basin and tub are draining? This house is an old house and much of the aboriginal plumbing has never been replaced; that means lead piping, possibly toxic, dating from about 1919. What if the whole building has to be re-piped? Oh God, no, not that! How do they work down from ceiling to floor to downstairs ceiling to basement? Will they have to go into the walls? The pipes, the pipes in the walls! Bronson and Viv have been reluctant to face such a crisis in their affairs, though they are meticulous about observing schedules for, say, root canal work. They can't handle the aggravation. But this Monday morning they invited Mayo Marcoux of Lafrenière Plumbing and Heating to come and have a cosmetic go at the bathroom basin drain. Bronson had been awakened – on Monday morning – by an apocalyptic thumping and pumping sound like that made by dinosaurs warring in the primeval ooze. Mayo, a plumber of Herculean force, was going at the basin drain with his biggest rubber plunger. First a squashing noise and then a sucking noise, whump, whump, whump, at 7:30 a.m. This dire sound had brought Bronson out of a light reluctant doze into alert waking. He knew without thought who was making the noise, with what instrument and for what purpose. It was – could only be – the sound of a tall plumber in the prime of life, let loose in a small bathroom to assault a blocked drain.

The operation continued for another hour during which Bronson choked down his customary light breakfast and assembled his materials for the day's work. Just before he left the house, a much-relieved Viv had shown him a clotted mass of gummy hair about the size of a softball, drawn from the trap under the basin. He recoiled, then was cheered by the appearance of Mayo on the staircase landing, beaming with satisfaction and brandishing his plunder like the great sword Durendal of Roland or Arthur or some other epic hero.

'Freed her right up! *Y'a encore de blocage pour sur.*'

Bronson hoped that the omission of the negative particle *pas* was purely idiomatic. When he finally got off to the office he left Viv with Mayo, comfortably seated in the breakfast nook drinking coffee and exchanging tales of heroic plumbers' adventures, of epic cost-estimates, and of work-orders eventually exceeded epically. No wonder that he had regressed into the tub as soon as he got home! And there she stood accusingly in the doorway. Problems!

Oh now, forever, he thought, farewell the tranquil mind. Farewell content. Farewell the plumèd troop and the big wars. Bronson's occupation's gone.

'Problems?' he quavered.

'Can't you hear?' said Viv, stamping her foot.

And indeed he heard the rush of water through the walls and the kitchen ceiling. Wordsworth, he thought irrelevantly, and smiled, and she grimaced as if in pain. 'We'll have to empty the water from the tub into the toilet. I think the toilet piping is O K,' she said.

Bronson rose from the tub like some old Triton or sea-god. Instead of a wreathed horn, Vivie handed him a plastic bucket and gave him simple instructions. 'We can't let the water out of the tub in any other way. If you pull the plug we'll have a tubful of dirty water …'

'… not *that* dirty …'

'… running along the kitchen counters. Already the ceiling is mush.'

He got to work while she phoned the plumbers' office. Filling the toilet bowl with water, flushing it, re-filling it, flushing it down again. He flung over his shoulder at Viv, 'Tell them not to let Mayo loose at the pipes again.' This admonition fell on deaf ears. In forty-five minutes the whole expensive team appeared, four of them, with M. Lafrenière personally in command. It must be serious, Bronson saw. M. Lafrenière never left the office. Dinner was ruined. The water had to be spooned and sponged from the kitchen counters, floor, walls, and then the ripping of the walls, the breaking into the ceiling.

The Bronsons went around the corner for Szechwanese, a cuisine which in Bronson's disturbed state was bound to act destructively on the lining of his digestive tract. He began to suffer from stomach pangs even before the hot sour sauce. He ought to have known better, said Viv.

'But dammit, you suggested this place.'

'I may have done, but I didn't force you to make a pig of yourself.'
She was feeling the pressure too.

When they got back to the house about 8:30, the sights that met
their eyes were piteous. Drip-cloth all over the kitchen, mouldings
ripped from the framing of the kitchen cupboards, a long strip of
wall opened up above the cabinets to reveal the course of the flood.
A third of the ceiling gone, and the offending pipes plainly revealed,
where they descended from above.

'Mayo ruptured it with his plunger,' said M. Lafrenière with
fatherly pride. 'That guy, he's very strong. See, see, if you look up
there you can see the hole in the pipe. That's all old pipe in there
that's gotta come out.'

'What, the whole house?' This was the calamity which the Bronsons had feared for so long. Possibilities of bank loans danced in
their heads. Eight thousand, ten thousand, four-year repayment
plans. Sell one of the GICs?

'Naw. Not the whole house. Just the linkage from the bathroom
down through here.' He indicated the line of the drainpipe with a
casual hand. 'We've got it all opened up now. You want to see
upstairs?' The followed him mutely to the second floor, around past
the bathroom door into a bedroom where a wooden hatchway had
been removed from the interior of a closet to reveal the backs of
basin and tub, and a hole through to the kitchen below.

'Those old builders, they knew what they were doing, you bet,'
said the master plumber approvingly. 'This house has got to be
seventy-five years old. Nowadays they just seal everything up and
you can't get at a leak without busting in. Here we've got this opening; we don't have to break hardly anything and we can section the
pipe and put in new, no problem.'

Mayo's enormous rump filled the space provided by the hatch.
There were sawing noises and a muffled voice which asked them to
adjust the work light. A definitive crunching sound. A wise man has
proposed that no other pleasure in life is as enchanting as that of
breaking lead pipe. It may be so. Mayo withdrew from the hole and
held up his trophy, a three-foot section of ancient tubing coloured
superbly by the dirt of three-quarters of a century, a dull bluish-
green.

'Here's your leak,' he said, pointing to a long irregular slit down one side of the excised member. Bronson thought that the object resembled a lacerated bowel. His stomach quivered sympathetically. 'Can't use your bathroom this week, maybe next week,' said M. Lafrenière, leading the Bronsons downstairs. 'But you've got a shower and toilet in your cellar, correct?' This was so. It seemed as though they would have to camp out for some time, trying their best to ignore the ravaged bathroom and its unfamiliar odour of exposed pipe and dank slime. 'You could use the toilet in there but you might not want to,' said the boss as he led them on a last look around the second floor. 'We're going to use the best quality new pipe, meets all building code provisions, will last a lifetime. We'll have a crew here day after tomorrow. It's a small job, shouldn't take more than three days. You'll be back in your tub by Friday.'

This was an inaccurate estimate. They were able to use the tub on a Friday, but not the Friday of the first week nor yet the second. It was a full nineteen days before the plumbing repair was complete. Other larger jobs took priority. The plumbers might come for an hour or two, tinker with pipe and sealant and the fittings under bathtub and basin, then be gone for what seemed an eternity but was usually a couple of days. They never forgot their tools or had to go back to the shop for more than ninety minutes at a stretch. They just didn't seem to be able to stay in the house for more than ninety minutes at a stretch. And while three of them were always present at any given moment of work, only two of them worked at a time. A third participant, not always the same person, seemed to hold a watching-brief only. At length, however, the repairs to the pipe and its connections were completed. Mayo filled the bathtub and basin and emptied them through the new connections on the afternoon of the nineteenth day as the Bronsons watched. Not a drip escaped the fine new pipe and its joints. The plumbers prepared to depart in good order, recovering their drip-cloths and tools and reinserting the hatch cover in the bedroom. 'We'll bill you,' said Mayo joyfully.

'Hey, but what about the opening in the kitchen ceiling?' This was a hole five feet by three and a half, impossible to ignore.

'For that you call your plasterers,' said one of the plumbers as the gang of three marched steadily down the front steps.

This tense command bothered Bronson more than any other aspect of the situation. In their twenty-five years in the house they had only once employed a plasterer, an ancient man dead these many years. Was a plasterer truly what was needed? Wouldn't some sort of small repairs contractor fit the bill better? Would it be a good idea to leave a hatch cover over the hole in the ceiling, in case they had to get in there again?

This suggestion proved to be Bronson's most valuable contribution to the exercise, money excepted. A removable countersunk panel, made of finest plywood and fitted into the ceiling with craftsmanly neatness, proved the perfect solution to the question of ceiling reconstitution. Stanley the small repairs man, whose panel truck bore no indication of his professional activities, and who accepted no payment not in currency (a discovery of Viv's), and a prompt and tactful worker, fitted in the panel in the course of two hours on a Saturday afternoon. He attached the panel with large, shiny, highly visible screws which were square-headed.

'In case you ever need to get back in there,' he said, looking down from the kitchen chair on which he was standing. This whole incident actually gave Bronson pleasure. The plywood was an unusual pinkish-brown colour which almost matched the existing ceiling paint.

'Then when you repaint,' said Stanley, stepping down from the chair, 'a single coat might cover, but be sure you clean the ceiling up good before.' He craned his neck and examined his installation with pride. 'Neat fit,' he said as Bronson handed him two hundred dollars in small unmarked bills. 'Call if you need anything else.' He scribbled his phone number on a scrap of paper. 'I don't give this out to just anybody,' he said. 'Be in touch.'

Bronson saw the good man to the door. Then he went back to the kitchen and gave the floor a careful sweeping. He looked up at the ceiling; the existing paint really went well with the new plywood.

All that was years ago and they've never repainted and now the 'new' ceiling panel can hardly be distinguished from the rest of the surface. Time the disguiser. Kindly Time.

A Subject for Thomas Hardy

Opal and Dennis Risley are doing fine; the marriage works. Three sons, twenty-one, eighteen, sixteen, never any trouble. A realty office in an immense suburb famous for fine restaurants and fifty square miles of residential properties, starter homes, single-family half-acre estates. A market like an ocean, rising and falling in tidal sequences that no woman can fathom and no man either. There's no gender discrimination in this business; they're in it together. Dennis manages the sales force and Opal handles accounting, billing and records. Five years ago she took a useful series of courses in programming and computer-use at the community college. Dennis knows nothing about the subject; he's perfectly happy to leave that to Opal. He says that there is a lot of information that she needs to have but is useless to him and the sales force. Most of the sales force are women, so the judgement isn't prejudicial. Sales people don't need to be on top of market trends; all they have to know is what the property will bring this morning. You can't close a sale by computer; it's a very personal event.

Opal doesn't feel buried in accounting and records like some dumb teenager. She has the business at her fingertips; she knows things nobody else even suspects, certainly not Dennis. He says he doesn't care what she's got on him. This is an unreadable compliment. He is an opaque man. Jolly. Likes to spend money. Has never made an abusive or dismissive gesture in her direction. Is not crazy about close physical contact. Who is he fooling?

She has trouble telling what he's thinking. When they go to one of their favourite restaurants it's as though Dennis was acting in a play. Greets the maître d'hôtel like a brother, has once discussed a deal with him, term-lease frontage in a distant mall. Got the maître d'hôtel out of a dubious commitment to a diminishing market. Now that mall is a desert of vacant boutiques and signs saying 'Seventy-percent off!' Now they greet each other with bear-hugs, salutes. The maître d' conducts them to their table, opens menus for them, offers sensible advice. There's a recession on, you can't depend on anything. Princess Diana has left her husband. What next?

As they leave the restaurant Dennis hands her the Visa slip for the records. She tucks it away and makes a mental note to access the expenses records in the morning with the entry. The meal won't cost them anything; they may even show a tiny profit on having gone out to eat. Same with the car, a two-year front-end lease with a dodgy buy-back arrangement. It would be hard to tell, at any time in the twenty-four-month rental agreement, who really owns the vehicle, the dealer, the lending body, certainly not the user. Property has turned into a welter of short-term leases; the way to wealth and fame lies through the dark forest of leasehold, building hotels with other people's money on Boardwalk and Park Place. No long-term commitment; the game only lasts for three hours.

Those slaps and embraces exchanged with tax inspectors make Opal wonder. They are just like Dennis in the bedroom, apparently jolly and warm, profoundly noncommittal. It seems as though he were somewhere else. There's nothing about him that she couldn't access but he has things on his mind.

Often after one of these high-cost/no-cost dinner dates he seems pleased with her, with himself. Done it again, he must be thinking, eaten my fill, drunk what I pleased (he drinks very moderately and has never been under the influence), paid nothing. May come out ahead. They get home around eleven on Thursday night; the boys may be anywhere. They certainly aren't at home. Dennis strolls before her into the master-bedroom suite. There's a spacious sitting-room with cosy fireplace, an enormous and technically sophisticated bathroom with mysterious taps, and a wide airy bedroom with ample closets. Foam rubber has never been allowed to intrude here. They both despise it. Two super-queen-sized beds, view of the river and the college campus in the distance. Opal decorated the house and Dennis is proud of her demonstrated taste. It's a welcoming, warm, cleanly room, almost one-hundred-percent free of allergic dust. They share a slight tendency to sinus complaints.

The curtains drawn, the tactful lighting partly shadowing the quiet space, some sort of mitigated passionate gesture seems permissible. They've been together for twenty-three years. Another couple

might long ago have gone their separate ways towards separate bedrooms and divided lives. Not Opal and Dennis. He welcomes her
jovially into his arms, wraps her (like the maître d'hôtel) in a big
hug. She can smell the skin of roasted duckling basted in orange
sauce, a smell that she enjoys. It must be on her; he had the fish.
They lie together for a while: neither is particularly sleepy. It's like
they're in public, or at a rehearsal for a closing or doing something
out of an instruction manual, by the book.

He tells her about her thick creamy skin. Little clicking people,
she thinks. She can hear the faint whir of the apparatus that cleans
and dampens the air in the house. Feels his hand moving very gently
down the length of her right thigh, a mildly agreeable, faintly questionable sensation. Not that there is anything indecent or suggestive
about the movement. It's more like some sort of paid skit. She can't
explain this to herself. Her women friends envy her and are
impressed by Dennis, and so they should be. They think it's amazing
that he has surrendered computer-literacy to her. It is a way of recog-
nizing the ascendancy of women in today's business world. Marvellous to have a husband who knows nothing about computers, when
she has the whole operation on ROM diskette. They tell her with glee
that a wife can't testify against her husband. This remark has been
made more than once and she finds it very unpleasant. After all, what
does she know?

She repeats to herself: I know nothing. A faint contrastive phrase
echoes back. I am innocent. I know nothing. What she knows she
can do is read and screen, note the responses, keyboard further
requests for information. More than once she has told herself that
she has all of Dennis in the box, on the screen, on diskette. She
knows more about residential real-estate prices than anybody in the
region, about imminent market trends, about yesterday's prices and
today's, about the likelihood of sudden movement at this or that
plateau. Thinks of courses in marketing. Not so much in taking them
as giving them. She knows everything except what Dennis is thinking. Her possession of secret knowledge brings her friends into the
office. They trust her, believing that asking and selling prices are
more accurately tracked in the Risley office than in the chain realtors'
sleazy storefronts. You only have to look at Opal as she sits beside her

terminal to know that she's in touch with the morning's market movement. Hazel and Bernie Cheung bought their last house in a seller's market six years ago, paying top dollar for an almost-new family residence with all conveniences in an exclusive location close to shopping districts and schools, yet secluded on a winding crescent that strangers find difficult to locate and follow to its dead-end. That was when the Cheung kids were in their mid-teens and the family needed room to spread out. Enormous room in the dazzlingly finished basement, laundry room, dad's combined study and office with air conditioning and built-in security installations, extra guest bedroom and fully-fitted basement bathroom. Ground-level L-shaped living and dining area fitted with oak flooring and traditional Bokhara carpeting, powder-room in the entryway, library, kitchen and back pantry, mud room, indoor access to three-car garage.

Upstairs is a palace, five bedrooms, master bedroom with bath en suite, two other bathrooms, fantastic closet space, airing cupboard. Now the kids are grown and living in distant provinces or in Europe or in Beijing. The Cheungs are rattling around in a house far too big for them. In today's economic climate they're spending four times what they need to on shelter. Better sell the house, take the capital-gains exemption, and move into a two-bedroom apartment, invest the realized capital, and Bob's your uncle.

Risley's First Rule: never discuss price during the client's opening appointment.

Opal can't remember whether she wrote this rule or Dennis did, but it's a goodie. Many times they've headed off unrealistic customer thinking about asking prices, and gotten a quick sale at a price advantageous to all parties. Nowadays there need be no guessing involved. You keyboard all relevant information about the property, omitting no detail however slight, and you get a printout that tells you what the house will bring, not last week, not yesterday, but this minute. Information is updated hourly, and nobody can access it but those whose modems interface with the database line. There have been one or two cases of hacker intrusion, but no erasures and no serious exploitation of the information. Hackers want circuitry, not property.

When a couple of friends come into the office and see Opal sitting beside the screen, their first impulse is to talk price. The Cheungs bought at the top of the curve; they'll expect a modest profit, but they won't get one. They'll have to be persuaded to ask what they paid for the house and accept a lower figure. Opal remembers the price they paid, four twenty-five. The Cheungs expect her to be able to bring that right back, but nobody uses her own memory any more. 'Circuit's down,' she says brightly, 'but Dennis will talk to you about it.' She doesn't like to put them off, but has never flouted Risley's First Rule and would be afraid (frightened, terrified, very reluctant, unable to bring herself) to do so. It must be Dennis's rule. Neither of them has even considered talking price to friend or enemy without prior discreet consultation. Dennis won't talk on any kind of telephone about prices, especially cellular phones.

'Three seventy-five?'

'They'll be taking a loss.'

'It's a paper loss and could be a hell of a tax break.'

'They want the capital for investment.'

'Could we sell them a condo?'

'They're talking apartments; there are vacancies everywhere.'

The condo market is holding steady but there isn't much movement. You can't find tenants for even the most luxurious apartment space at favourable rents. Where have all the apartment dwellers gone?

'They wouldn't care to invest in an apartment building?'

Opal knows that she needn't answer this. Dennis never asks a question to which he doesn't know the answer.

'We'll get them to open at the price they paid. Let them sweat a bit. They bought at the top of the market; there's nothing to be done about it.'

'We might finally get them four twenty-five.'

'We might have to wait a year to collect our sixty-five seven.'

'It was four hundred half an hour ago.'

'They can't possibly know that.'

'Should we tell them?'

'We're paying a high price for privileged information.'

'But it's part of our customer service.'

'I think we start them off at four twenty-five, Opal?'

'They won't really lose by it?'

'It's a very tough market?'

'I guess you're right?'

'You know I'm right?'

'We're the experts. Aren't we?'

'That's what we're here for?'

This is all discussed at their second meeting with their friends the Cheungs, who are disappointed to find that their fine big house is worth less than they paid for it, getting on for seven years ago. That was when home owners were in their most comfortable position in recent times. Only professional athletes and a few entertainers have seen the price of their services rise significantly over this period. House property has steadily declined in value but home owners refuse to accept this. Why haven't property taxes declined? They've swallowed tax increases every year and put up with them because they believed they would recover the tax inflation when they came to sell the house. Now they find that the property is not worth what they gave for it and their most recent tax bill shows a four-percent increase. There's something wrong somewhere.

'Now they want to go to market value assessment,' says Bernie Cheung, 'and they'll do it too, if this government doesn't show some initiative.' He says this coming out of Dennis's office, and looks protestingly at Opal as he passes her desk. She sits right out there in public, giving an impression of openness and scientific precision. She smiles at Bernie and Hazel and bends her head towards the screen. Her image smiles back at her secretly. She taps the keys click click. End of second appointment, a listing at four twenty-five.

Now the Risleys confer. It is fairly clear from the stream of price quotations fed out from their database that the Cheungs can expect two or three offers at four ten within ten days. Should they be encouraged to wait that long? Opal looks at Dennis. She suspects something but isn't sure what.

'I can move it tomorrow at three seventy-five?'

'Oh, you devil. You've got a buyer at that price, haven't you?'

He refuses to say anything.

'Haven't you?'

When he looks at her like that she feels something unusual. She knows what's coming, secrets. She hates this. He's got a hand-picked buyer hidden away somewhere halfway across the city. Some unknown speculator who wants to pick up the property at a sweet-heart figure and roll it over for a quick morning's profit. All he has to do is persuade Hazel and Bernie to let it go for the quick sale at three seventy-five. That isn't going to be easy.

Opal: 'No, honestly, we can have a firm offer on the table by eleven o'clock at that figure ...'

Bernie: 'It's a hell of a figure. You're asking us to take a fifty-thou-sand-dollar chop.'

Hazel: 'Wait a minute, Bernie. I'm sure Opal wouldn't ask if it wasn't important. Would you, Opal?'

Opal: 'That's what the printout projects for the next three months. Why wait till then? The market may still be falling. Dennis thinks we're heading into a recession or worse.'

Bernie: 'Can I see that printout?'

It's a prepared printout for a house with one less bedroom, one less bathroom, a two-car garage and no extras, but who can tell? She hands it over and her friends can't read it anyway, the text is very grey.

Hesitations, mutterings; they confer in the doorway. Hazel nodding her head and looking over her shoulder at Opal. She is persuading him on her girlfriend's say-so. When they come back in, Opal says gloomily, 'We'll take a loss of seventy-five hundred on the commission.' This is accurate, and Dennis has asked her to be sure to work it in.

Two days later she instructs support staff to prepare papers, the firm offer and the acceptance are in the file, and only the acceptance requires signature. Bernie and Hazel are coming over around 2:15 to sign the acceptance. Dennis will be there. He likes to attend as many signings as he can; it means something for the vendor to have the salesman present. He's the sole liaison between buyer and seller, after all, the only contact they have prior to closing. Perhaps this is just as well.

Anyway, they're all of them sitting around the big table in the directors' room (Dennis and Opal are the directors of record) and

Hazel is in the middle of signing the agreement forms – she's the nominal owner of the property – when one of the staff brings the day's mail in for Opal to go through, mostly flyers, and one long, lean, unmarked legal-sized envelope with no letterhead and yesterday's postmark.

Hazel finishes signing the copies. She straightens up and hands the pen back to Dennis.

Bernie says something under his breath.

They all turn and look at Opal as the flap loosens on the envelope and then flips free. She slides out a stiffish piece of paper and turns it over. A certified cheque made out to Dennis in the amount of twenty-five thousand dollars. Indecipherable signature, non-committal note attached by a copper-coloured paper clip. Dennis has netted seventeen thousand, five hundred, for less than an hour of doing nothing.

Something is happening to Opal's skin; she is wearing a light summer dress and can see the skin on her upper chest changing colour. Her face tingles. Blood rises in her cheeks. They're staring at her. They can tell! She certainly is feeling something unusual. What's it called?

Deconstruction

Meaning leaps off maps into life.

Imagine the Three I League, then recreate its spread on a map of the Midwest. Indiana, Illinois, Iowa, were the three I's. The cities of the league come to the eye from the tiny lettering in their natural configuration: Evansville, Decatur, Peoria, Moline, Cedar Rapids, Des Moines, but not Indianapolis, which was bigger than these other places and wouldn't have fitted into the limited budgets permitted Class B teams. Cities in the Three I League were all in the same range of population and prosperity. They all had some very good reason for being where they were, and were all within an overnight bus-ride of each other. When you look at the map with the history of baseball in the Midwest in mind, the Three I League rises out of nonentity into memory and from there into abundant meaning. What you can recover from maps!

Connections and lines of force, the reason Moline is where it is, or the spidery line of an old railway on the map. Now look at this sheet. Here's the ghost of a line that used to run from Stoverville through Forfar Junction to Westport, the SWLS. You can trace the life of the region, hanging from the spiderline like stiffly dried clothing pinned to a wire swinging in the wind. Stoverville, Athens, Delta, the Junction off in the fields, no town very near, only the walls of the celebrated cheese factory visible near the highway across eight wide fields.

Junctions propose investigations; mysteries hide under the inscribed crossing; it's marvellous to ponder the meeting of two insistent systems of behaviour. Could trains turn from the SWLS onto the CN? Could an engineer start from Stoverville, arrive at the Junction, then choose not to continue to Newboro and Westport, but to deviate towards Chaffee's Locks and Sydenham? Were the connecting tracks arranged in cloverleafs, allowing passage from one line to another? Was there a roundhouse at Forfar Junction, or was branch-line traffic destined for eternity to travel along one line but never the other? Couldn't you get from Stoverville to Chaffee's Locks without changing trains? You can do it easily in a car.

I shouldn't let my girlfriend see maps; they unsettle her. She has to go and find out the answers to these puzzles. As soon as we'd picked out the crossing of the two lines on our government maps, she dragged me out there to look over the ground, search for relics of derelict platforms and waiting-rooms, ways to change your destination. Maybe you could descend from the up train from Athens, wait for your connection, catch the down train from Smith's Falls and eventually arrive at Perth Road or Sydenham. Triumph of a specific cultural form! You used to be able to make trips like these all over England until Doctor Beeching tore up the branch-line system in 1963 and inflicted a ghastly wound on the fabric of British society. In the old times, in Britain, you could get anywhere from here if you were content to put in a spot of junction-sitting time. The ballplayers in a Class B league went by bus from Evansville to Des Moines, riding overnight on two-lane highways in vehicles without lavatories. Every system of travel links has its own corollaries: the 2:00 a.m. toilet stop, with coffee.

Staring at the spiderlines on the fine map, we felt that we must go there at once. The Junction! Wide skies, huge empty fields, strong lines of trees stretching away in perspective alongside the southwest-bound CN trackage. The simple metal cross that allowed intersection plain in the packed crushed stone. We stood on either side of the meeting-point admiring the simplicity and elegance of the small gaps in the rails that allowed the crossings.

At the same time we had to curse and condemn the disappearance of all the rest of the rails from one of the lines, the SWLS, which had been taken away fifty years before. What a loss, what a wrong it had been to place the line under erasure, leaving only the connecting CN rails in place, the intersecting trackage still linking Smith's Falls to the virgin back-country around the Rideau Lakes, to Sydenham, to Kingston. At least, we told each other, at least they're planning to do something with the tracks that have survived.

You have to envision the quality of the place. We'd been able to drive almost to the spot where we now stood; an almost vanished access road still leads from the highway to the Junction. People used to come here in Gray Dorts and Studebakers to pick up arriving relatives or to speed them on their way. You could easily get to Ottawa from here, or Kingston or Stoverville or Westport, a whole region, eastern Ontario, brimming with life, with an impressive history and this lonely deserted crossing at its precise centre. We were standing in the middle of gone timeliness, sunk in deep temporality beyond happening, and the wind whistled its message of loneliness and evanescence. The line from Stoverville all overgrown, the rails from Smith's Falls starting to rust though they'd only gone out of use two years ago and looked able to handle heavy new traffic. Meanwhile the leaves rattled in the moving air and we stared round-eyed at each other, troubled by absence.

'Well, anyway, they're reactivating the CN tracks.'

'So they tell you,' I said to her, 'but who are they?'

'We'll make a booking for the first trip, won't we?'

'We'll be first in line. It's such a great idea!' We'd learned from the papers that a group of private investors had applied to the Commission in Ottawa for permission to reopen the line and run twice-daily excursion trains between Smith's Falls and Kingston, one down, one up, a distance of maybe seventy-five miles, say a hundred and thirty kilometres as the rails wound through the lake district and across swamps. Depart Smith's Falls at 6:30 p.m. and enjoy cocktail service, happy hour on wheels, as your luxuriously appointed lounge-car pulls away into the setting sun at a comfortably leisurely pace. No point in disturbing the ballast on the old roadbed. Just a nice soft run, taking our time, expecting twilight to enfold us somewhere around Forfar Junction, slowdown at the crossing-point so the punters can admire the scenic beauties of this lonely spot.

Then as twilight deepens, your Exploring Eastern Ontario Excursion Run probes the mysterious recesses of Rideau Canal country, as your gourmet meal is served in the adjacent restaurant car. By the time you get to the steel bridge at Chaffee's Locks you're four courses and two wines into a spectacular eight-course repast. The lakes and rivers and rock shelves and railway apparatus slide stealthily past the windows, spectral in the growing dark, but the brave lights from dining- and bar-car windows throw a momentary brightness over harsh terrain unchanged in appearance since human beings appeared in the place at some unknowable past time. If we keep on an easy thirty miles an hour – there being no other traffic on the line but the sister train northbound – we can make the run last nearly three hours, arriving Kingston just as the last mille-feuilles and the last snifter of brandy are consumed. What a way to go, it'll catch on big! And we'll be on the first downbound run. We'll leave the car at Smith's Falls and pick it up the next night after the return trip. How do you think the food might be? Might be better-than-average dining-car fare. Might rise almost to connoisseur quality. Might even have a decent wine list, and at slow speeds the wine should travel well. What a good idea for a summertime excursion package! Romantic!

But would the Commission go for it? Maybe it's too good to live. This is no country for good ideas.

So we're standing at the intersection of two railway lines, one gone forever, the other hanging in abeyance. We've come to see if they're doing anything to restore them to elegant, lively, entertaining use. We look at each other happily, thinking of well-trained food-service staff, job-creation, revival of an industry and a region; they won't like it, not one little bit. We can sense this powerfully; but who are they and what have they got up their sleeves?

We knew when we read about it that all the forces of reaction and gloom would marshal themselves against the idea of gourmet meals served in the wilderness on a slow train to Kingston. It was too bright an idea; it never had a chance. We thought we'd better go and see what was being done; all the rails required was a bit a rust-removal and a few new spikes. And there we were, a hundred yards from our car in the middle of nowhere, the breeze rising and falling, making the only sound for miles. Or no, there was something else, away off up the line, scissors-grinding? No. Something dinging in the fields. A ball? What?

'What is that thing up there? It's moving. I can hear something. Can't you see?'

She's very insistent, my girlfriend.

I strained my eyes to look, and she was dead right. About two miles up the line to the northeast there was some very large moving thing making a faint clanging sound and moving towards us very slowly, maybe five miles an hour. At that rate it would take whatever it was about an hour to reach us. We were expecting to have a little picnic anyway, so we decided to wait and see what was coming at us. I thought it might be one of those rail-sharpening cars you used to see around way stations, or some maintenance vehicle. But why would it be making that noise? Clang. It was exactly that, a clang, a real metallic echoing ring but not shrill like a bell. Lower in pitch and resonant.

'Beats me.'

She said, 'They're doing something to the rails.' How would she know?

'Eat your sandwich,' I said, 'you made it.' They were good sandwiches, though not like an eight-course gourmet meal served with three or four wines. We had juice and coffee in a pair of big thermos bottles. The clanging getting louder as we ate. I did not like the sound at all; it reminded me of unpleasant things. It had a warlike sound. I stood up and walked over to the junction points and looked at what was coming. It was much closer now, about a mile off. It looked like a huge bug, and while it wasn't moving fast it certainly wasn't stopping for anything. I wouldn't have wanted to get in its way. Now it was less than half a mile off; it just kept coming, and at a quarter of a mile I could see that it had a sort of low, pointed ram-bow at the front, like some old battleship left over from the First World War, or like an armoured train. And it had terrible wings.

At three hundred yards, seeming to move a little quicker, it was making an awful noise and it looked like a dragon or a giant beetle or something out of the Apocalypse, snouted, armoured, almost completely inhuman. It seemed to have a solitary driver, sitting up at the front at a control panel in a shielded compartment, directing the motion of the wings. Sometimes they lay couched alongside the body of the vehicle; sometimes they rose up sidewise, showing huge clawing grippers that might have been magnetized. They took a sure hold on whatever they seized, and only let go when the operator threw a switch and de-magnetized them. The noise was rising to enormous volume. On either side of the beetle the huge wings would fold down tight behind the rear wheels and seize the rails over which they had just passed. There would be a wrenching tugging motion in the clawing wings; then they would rise up and away from the sides of the giant car, each one with a rail in its clutch, torn from the ballast and the ties, scattering spikes and coarse gravel in a hard solid rain. The wings would shake the rails in their clutches, then swing them out and away from the car, dropping them with the clanging thudding sound we'd heard from far off.

The steel rails might have been toothpicks or matchsticks hanging from the devouring claws; it was a terrible sight. The noise was enough to send you off your head and the look of the car was unearthly. I'd never seen anything like it before. I didn't suspect there were such things in the world, destructive, obliterating and irresistible. I realized that I was standing too close to the crossing and that I could be crushed by falling steel. I retreated to a safe distance and put my hands tightly over my ears as the beast, monster, leviathan, came alongside.

I couldn't blot out the sound, which was now overwhelming. I shouted, almost shrieked at the goggled figure seated high above me in his cab. I waved my arms, trying to signal to the driver, but there was no response – the only time I can recall a railway-crew failing to acknowledge a salute from the ground. The muffled figure looked neither to left nor to right, just urged the destroyer on its way. I had to fall back a considerable distance to avoid being struck by a falling rail or a flying spike. I was fifty yards from the right of way when I realized that my girlfriend had disappeared. She had to be across the tracks; she's a smart woman who wouldn't just stand there inviting her death-blow from a flying piece of steel. But I couldn't see or hear her. There was nothing in my head but the sound of the thing's forward motion and the impression made by the falling tracks. I felt very frightened.

Now the vehicle was just at the junction point, where the two lines had met and crossed; some obstruction seemed to block its forward movement. The great metal wings seized and ground to a halt, as though the power had been cut off. They hung half-lifted in the air, and great chunks of earth fell from them directly on the crossing. Twice the car gave a hitching shifting lurch. I saw that the driver was trying to pass over the intersection point without taking up the pieces of metal that formed it. I felt a superstitious dread when I saw this, as if some form of evil worship was being invoked. The noise started up again and the wings flapped horribly, and the operation went forward, moving towards the southwest and the lake district with awful persistence.

As it cleared the intersection it started to catch up the useless metal more strongly than before. I had to dodge and retreat as a long flying thing fell right in front of our car. I hopped backwards in fright, and then as the noise receded I heard my girl calling to me.

'Look out, you idiot, do you want to get yourself killed?'

I felt relieved. I wouldn't care what she said to me as long as she was all right. She was holding the empty picnic basket in her arms. She'd been standing on the other side of the tracks when the rail-grabber went by, in perfect safety but out of sight and inaudible. Nobody could have made themselves heard over that noise. I joined her at the point where the two lines had met and there, sure enough, were the crosspieces and the points of the junction, but all the rails were displaced. We looked to one side and the other; the embankment was all tossed and tumbled, opened by the passing of the huge car like a scalpel wound in a naked torso. There were dirty spikes all over the place. Even the heavy, oiled and blackened ties, those mighty baulks, were dislodged and twisted into bizarre positions.

'Somebody's going to have to clean all this up,' she said.

'I don't know. I think they may just leave it like this. What an awful thing to do. What a mess!'

We walked a few hundred feet up the line, looking over the transformed scene. The rails lay scattered at various angles in the earth and weeds to either side of the embankment. Tons of metal cast in the specific form for this – and only this – use, lying abandoned and obscured in the rising dust. The ground seemed to shudder under our feet. Perhaps this was only a vibration communicated through the ground by the rail-grabber as it headed off southwest, making its special noise, overriding all things, heading for the secret lakes and rock ridges in the deep back country. At its slow determined pace the unpurged image of destruction on wheels went on its way, unwinding the meaning of a hundred and fifty years, which must now sink back into the lines of an old map, and from there to nonentity.

A Gay Time

Sproule Kincaid was seconded to the department from on high without our request, probably to observe and smooth over some disputes that had been simmering around the fax terminal for a while. That's where the crowd swarms in mid-morning, when you want to get inter-city communications out of the way before lunch, especially at the beginning of the week. Five or six of us middle-level staff used to get backed up in there waiting our turn. The mere child who was supposed to operate the machine was clumsy and forgetful, and used to be in tears by coffee break on Tuesdays. There was plenty of casual bickering, and some in-office, cross-gender socializing, which I don't think is ever a good idea.

The department head brought this man around to the faxing centre on his first day and gave us the stuff about co-operation and making things easy for the new chum, and what his slot was on the organigram and other vague information. He didn't say anything very specific about what this guy was supposed to be doing or how long he might be among us. Good suit, I noticed, and not much to say for himself. No commitment there, I thought. Somebody who's not making any sudden revelations. I watched where they located his office space, and was impressed and a bit frightened. For a long time after that he didn't appear on the flow chart. You couldn't be sure where he fitted in. I suspected from the start that he didn't report to the department head, but to somebody higher up, maybe a long way up. He sometimes requested data on traffic flow, which is all collated next door, and sometimes about marketing and statistics, which is me. Us. There are thirty-seven of us in the section. I'm the next-to-youngest.

I could feel him keeping his eye on his neighbours; there was something creepy about it. He used to sit by himself in his room and desk-top without help from resident staff; he didn't seem to need assistance from anybody of the other gender. This in itself was an attention-getter. He seemed to believe that he could manage by himself. He had a modem in there, and almost infinite storage capacity. Never made any noise; he had a very quiet keyboard. He was storing something, that was plain. But what?

In any operation the size of ours there are always going to be redundant elements and bad consciences. If he was reporting on production and performance to a higher echelon you would have to predict some reductions in staff. But they didn't come, and they didn't come. It made us all nervous, like waiting for an electrical storm to start. I'm not working to improve the corporation's standing in the marketplace. I've got expenses to meet, my apartment and my clothes and my hair and upgrading my power and capacity and software. And my entertainment. I spend money on my lunches. I enjoy going to pricey sandwicheries and delis. It's good to be seen there. Nobody takes me. I buy my own and I'll usually go in a group of three. I never go for lunch by myself. I'm twenty-four. I've got my future to think about. I always feel I'm being watched.

When this Kincaid started to turn up at the Dundas Deli from time to time, I wondered about him. Nobody likes a spy, and anyway I had nothing to hide. And if he had his eye on me, I had mine on him too, you know.

He had this blade-like look as though you were seeing him in three-quarter profile with a firm jawline and very freshly shaved skin. You wondered about his home life. Around that time people's personal orientations were under close scrutiny. You had to be prepared to make a full disclosure of your assets and habits, who you saw and who your companions were. It was the time of the first big AIDS scare, which has of course continued up to now. It brought with it a complete reversal of our ideas about what was sexy. Sex stopped being sexy; you couldn't feel certain about anything. Romance became an obscene word and disappeared from magazine covers, also courtship, also boyfriend. You couldn't encourage anybody because you didn't know where they'd been last night or all those nights before. The whole thing's just poisoned love for me. I don't know where to look.

The whole thing was such a big cheat. Here we were supposed to have gotten freedom and equality for the first time in our history. Women could behave like men, choose their partners, have as many or as few – or none – as we liked. If you were gay or lesbian or chaste you didn't need to hide it. You could see whom you pleased, do what you felt like. Then came the big scare and nobody could trust anybody any more. By the time I was nineteen I was a very cynical woman. I didn't let anybody touch me and I was definitely not attracted to strangers. Attraction could be a smoking gun.

This Kincaid fellow suited the times, cold, silent, noncommittal. You could not ask him anything about himself, if he had a self. I watched him come and go and I waited for signs of bad behaviour, molestation, sexism, pawing, but they didn't come. I thought he was just a buttoned-up prick. I mean, what kind of a name is Sproule Kincaid? It sounded like the bad guy in a forties cowboy movie. He might as well have been called Snake Bastardly or something. You were sure he was up to no good, in some especially unpleasant way, but it never showed. He just collected bytes like fleas. I have to admit it, he was fascinating. I couldn't take my eyes off him whenever he stopped playing with his keyboard and passed through our section to go for a fax. He wore Harry Rosen suits. There are no Kincaids in the directory, or at least there weren't until last fall when his name turned up for the first time. A new listing, a bit of information gained against all odds. Suddenly he's in the book, the only Kincaid. Could he have changed his name, or was he operating under an a.k.a.? You had to wonder.

Mention of last fall makes me remember the Christmas party. Everybody allows that this is the right time for a little fun and games. You don't much like it, but you let the barriers down a little though not to the extent of exchange of body fluids or sharing of needles. Just kidding! I don't do any of that. But I have let people hold my hand at Christmas parties. Two years ago a much younger woman tried to take my hand when she was half smashed. I stamped that out in a hurry, you can bet. I looked at the poor little thing; her hair was out of control and she'd just been in the copy-centre with somebody. I think it was a man.

'I'm so lonely,' she whimpers in this little-girl voice.

I jerked my hand away and passed off the incident with a casual remark.

'I'm sorry,' I said. 'I hate to be touched.'

You'd have thought I'd insulted her. She went dead white and ran out of the office. There's no dealing with some people. I hadn't said anything to offend her, or criticized her look, which was bizarre when you studied it. Certain people just don't ever fit in. I thought I noticed Sproule (Sproule?) watching me across this big space. I hate a person with two last names. Stanley Nelson. Mackenzie Philips. Sproule Kincaid. Weird! Why wasn't he called something like Tom or Roy? I checked and was strangely pleased to find eight Sproule families in the book. There it is, I thought, he has two family names and no first name, or he's concealing it. Probably something ridiculous like Armbruster or Clarence. I felt that this was a major step forward in my investigations of Evil Sproule Kincaid. The trouble with surveillance is that it consecrates a relationship. It gets so you don't know who's maintaining surveillance and who's being surveyed, if that's the word I want. Maybe the best thing is to say nothing, see nothing and veer away from contamination. And don't use dirty needles. God, but I'm scared these days.

For about a year after that rotten Christmas party (I heard afterwards that the pale girl had vomited for half an hour in the loo) there was a consistent buzz in our section about Mr Kincaid. He had to be queer. He was straight. He was a switch-hitter. He was neutered in an unbecoming way. He was religious. He was out for what he could get. He was in the book. He had an unlisted number. I put this last rumour to sleep quick enough.

'He's in the book and if you dial the number you get a dial tone.'

'Guess who's been calling Mr Kincaid,' said our supervisor. I felt smirched and was miffed.

'He hasn't got an answering service yet,' I said.

'Oh ho, oh ho!'

There was laughter, which made me furious. I definitely do not like being laughed at; it's really unacceptable. And then one of the others nosed around and contacted his answering machine, or so she said.

'He must have just got it recently,' I said.

'Well, you'd be the one to know, wouldn't you?' I hate that sort of smart remark, and anyway his answering service was useless. When you called it you got the standard taped discourse:

Hello. You have reached 484-8550, and this is Mr Kincaid speaking. I'm unable to come to the phone at this time, but if you will leave a message at the end of the long beep I'll get back to you as soon as possible.

He never did get back to anybody. There was plenty of comment about that and not just in marketing and statistics either; there must have been dozens of calls. Nobody else of any known sex answered his phone, not a mother or sister or lover or friend or man or woman. Blank. Stonewalled. There was just no way of knowing, but we did have one thing to follow up, his address. He was middle-management at least. That meant large earnings and perhaps some successful investments. A loner like that might be doing pretty well. Whenever I got to that point in my thinking I used to turn myself off. There is no profit in thinking that way any more. Who could you allow to court you? Who could you love? The boy next door has HIV. You don't know, do you? I checked out his address one Sunday afternoon, and do you know, he had the whole second floor of a big luxurious old mansion on Spring Garden Road. The whole floor. Room for parties, or for wife and kids.

There was a separate entrance for the second-floor apartment, inside the front door off the veranda. I tiptoed in and looked at it carefully. It was a tight-fitting solid piece of wood that looked like oak. You couldn't hear a thing from the staircase. The only way you could identify the place as his was from the little card over the mail slot that said 'Kincaid 2-A'. I walked all around the house: all the second-floor windows were equipped with real shutters, and at the back some of them were half closed. They were open in front; you could see very neat curtains hanging to either side of each window. It looked like an eight-room apartment to me, with perhaps a couple of bathrooms, pretty luxurious. He couldn't be living there all alone, could he? He had to be living with somebody, but who? Girl, guy, old mother? Rumours were rife. I may have started some of them myself. My personal position was that he was gay, but very discreet about it. Somehow the exterior of his apartment didn't quite fit in with this estimate, but I thought it was the most likely one. He just didn't look like somebody who was living with a woman or even a wife. He had that sharp, poised, independent attitude. People will talk!

Nobody cares if you're gay, so long as you don't give them anything. I can barely remember when some older people acted turned off by gays and lesbians. When the epidemic hit, fifteen years ago there was some criticism of the gay lifestyle, but you never hear it any more; we've all grown up to it. There's no criticism attached to whatever it is you do; people just feel a natural curiosity, that's all. I thought I might try to bring him out of his shell a bit. Do him good. Once when I was on the over-the-top phase of a mood-swing I dug a favourite old dress out of my closet, something I hadn't worn for a year, too feminine. It was a dark silver colour in a lightweight silk, with a very pale parrot motif across it, white bird-like figures. It had a long skirt, almost three-quarter length, with tucks all around the waist, and a lot of material below the waist that floated out if you made a sudden turn. I looked about thirty. It wasn't really something you'd wear to the office or to the mall for lunch, but I thought I'd give it a whirl to see if I could get a reaction. Kind friends in the workplace were full of reactions, but it wasn't them I had in mind.

'Oooooooohhhhh, would you look at this?'

'I'm going somewhere at 4:30,' I said. I was really too dressed up to do anything. I hung out near Kincaid's door most of the day. I guess it was pretty obvious, but I was determined I'd get something out of him. Around 3:00 p.m. he popped out the door with his profile showing up nicely – the old blade-like look – and took a quick look at me.

'Nice dress,' he said, taking a big risk. There were witnesses. You can prosecute people for saying things like that in front of onlookers. Sexual harassment in the workplace is what that is. The first place you go is to the Human Rights Commission. I know women who've had to do that. Somebody speaks nicely to them and they have to have their revenge. If I were to answer I'd be encouraging unacceptable behaviour and he might say something worse.

'I'm glad you like it,' I said. It just slipped out. He took out a notebook and made an entry in it. Then he walked off in the direction of our supervisor's office. Could he be some kind of an investigator? Who were his associates? I could feel my skirt floating above my ankles, and sensed an unusual pleasure. Half an hour later he came back. Maybe he'd only gone to the washroom. I stepped in front of him when he went to go back into his office.

'Do you think it makes me look older?' I said. He didn't lose a stride, just dived into his lair like a hunted animal.

The next afternoon he accosted me by the elevators. 'Have you got a minute, Emily?' he said.

'Who told you my name?' I said. I hate my name.

'I have my methods,' he said.

'All right then, what's your real first name? Nobody's called Sproule. It's impossible.'

'That's really my middle name; it's my mother's family name. My first name, if you have to know is … well, it's Charlie.'

I felt myself gaping. Charlie and Emily. What a pair!

'Would you care to come around to my place for a drink tomorrow night?' said this old mystery man. 'I'm having one or two people in, nothing special, but there will be food, if that means anything.' What he was trying to say was that he was giving a party, the old devil, can you imagine? I wondered what sort of party. I don't do drugs and I like to keep all my clothes on and I don't do anything in groups of more than two.

'What time should I turn up?'

'Sevenish.'

Emily, for God's sake!

Naturally I couldn't keep away, but I did feel a little like Bluebeard's final wife on her way to have a look at the forbidden room, as I rang the buzzer beside the mailbox. You're a silly girl, I told myself as the buzzer sounded a reply, but I pulled the heavy door open and climbed the dark flight of stairs. The upstairs door must have been as thick and closely fitted as the front door; you couldn't hear a thing. It was like looking upwards into a cave.

Then all at once the door at the top of the stairs was flung open and the upper staircase shone with different coloured lights. Three big balloons came bouncing out the doorway, rebounded from the wall and floated down to me, a green one, an orange one, a pretty pink one. Pink for girls. I collected them in my arms and went into the foyer. There was music and changing lights and singing and a lot of chatter. Paper streamers. I clutched my balloons. One of them made a squeaky sound as darling Charlie came up to me smiling.

'I'm so glad you were able to come,' he said. I gave him the pink balloon and he batted it up at the high ceiling.

A lovely woman dressed in a way that made my mouth water strolled up to us. She blew on one of those party favours that unroll when you blow into them, making a whistling noise. There was a feather on the unrolling end of the little toy. Yellow. From some canary or other, I suppose. The feather caressed my right earlobe.

'Whoopee!' said this woman. I reached up and caught the pink balloon. Then she and Charlie and I linked hands and laughed; there were many other laughing people in the foyer. And I understood with what immense power tradition holds us in its grip.

A Catastrophic Situation

'Look at what her grandpapa has given her, isn't it sweet?' Chatterings from female cousins, throat-clearings from uncles, horrified speech in undertones in the gloomy old drawing-room.

'Fossette, where did you get this? Does he mean you to have it for your own?'

'Yes, mamma. He gave it to me just this minute, and he told me to bring it down to the family conclave. Con-clave. Is that right?'

'The old devil!'

'What's he doing up there? Why don't we have him declared incompetent?'

'Shhh. Ssshhhhh! The child will hear you. We're never sure how much she understands or what the old man says to her. And this is his house, and everything in it. We don't know what he's keeping up there. Fossette is the only one he allows in. Isn't that right, darling? Aren't you your grandfather's little playmate?'

'That's what he calls me, mamma, and his little protector and his assistant, and other things.'

'What sort of other things, dearest?' This from Aunt Hélène, the frightening one with the lace. 'Does he ever take you on his knee?'

'No. Never. He tells me he might dirty my dress with charcoal dust or colouring. He says he daren't touch me, but he loves me and wants me to remember how we love each other. That's why he made this drawing for me. I had to go up on the dais under the skylight and sit quietly on the model throne all morning. I wore my little cotton summer dress, the primrose one, and held my straw hat in my hands while he worked. I'd never been allowed to watch him work before. But now he says that I'm old enough but not too old. I don't quite know what he means, but he always laughs when he says that.'

'Know what he's done? This is a master drawing in his most finished late style.'

'And he's mounted it himself and framed it. Hasn't he framed it, Mathilde? Isn't that his work?'

'Yes, yes, yes, naturally it is. He wouldn't let a framer get his paws on something like this. It's exquisite. In his finest manner. I don't know what to say about it.' She turns to her daughter. 'And you're quite sure he didn't ask you to bring it to us for safekeeping?'

'No, mamma. He gave it to me; it's for my room, you see, for me to hang on the empty wall facing the armoire. I know it's only black and white, he said, but it'll brighten your little cabane, won't it? It's nice of grandfather to think of that.'

The work is handed very cautiously from aunt to uncle, and each one whistles or makes some smothered exclamation as it comes into their view, for the drawing is beyond valuation, a late work in pen and ink with washes and highlighting by Georges des Chénonceaux. Couldn't be by anybody else, the finest draughtsman of his time, admired by *both* Picasso and Bonnard, a double-first.

'He's fixed it ...'

'And he's signed it, "pour la petite Fossette", and dated it and written the date and time of mounting on the back.'

'He's even fitted the little screw eyes and the wire for hanging.'

'Fossette?'

'Yes, papa?'

'Now, my child, this is a very serious matter, an important matter. Is your grandfather working every day? Does he produce new things like this each time you see him?'

'No, papa. He sits and looks over sheets and sheets of things. Some of them he throws on the floor, and one or two he pins up. Then he takes them down too, and drops them on the pile. He talks to me while he does this.'

Fossette's Uncle Maurice shows painful interest in these remarks. He's a heavy-browed gloomy fellow, an attorney of some kind, who at one time handled the painter's contractual affairs. Now he grumbles, 'We must have an evaluation made before it's too late, and the old chap must revise his will. Do you understand what there is in the studio?'

And Uncle Maurice takes Fossette's new possession in his widespread hands. He cocks his head and examines the work minutely. 'I'm no evaluator. I don't buy pictures. I prefer to wait to inherit them. But I've been in the galleries, here and in Florence and London and in New York, and I know what this would fetch. Half a million. Look at that head. Look at the turn of the neck, how he's shaded it in with a single stroke of his pen. And the suggestion of the texture of the cotton, and the child's cheek, and those ribbons ...'

'Suggest a price,' says Fossette's father.

'Oh but, papa, it's mine. I'm not to sell it. Never.'

'Of course not, child, nothing of the kind. Your father is simply curious. It's a rare gift. It will have to be included in the insurance inventory.'

'Yes, mamma, but I'm to hang it in my room, isn't that so?'

'Yes, yes, dear. Listen to your Uncle Maurice.'

'But I want to take my picture to my room.'

'Yes, darling, of course. Go with her, Maurice, would you? Find a picture hook and help her to hang it. We can' (whispers) 'include it in the inventory another time.'

'I'll see to it.' The attorney takes the picture from a hovering aunt and moves towards the door.

'But I want to carry it. I'm big enough.'

'Give it to her, Maurice, but watch to see if she needs help.'

The relatives listen with attention as the ill-matched pair mount one of the back staircases.

II

When we got to the third floor I went one way and Uncle Maurice went another. He doesn't live in our house and doesn't know his way along the corridors, and besides, it's so dark up here. Mamma keeps the lights turned off; she says they're too expensive to burn all day and night. There aren't any windows along my corridor because it goes down the middle of the house and the rooms on either side have the windows, funny little windows, some of them are perfectly round. Then there are the branch corridors at either end of the house, that lead to the bathrooms and the wcs, one at each end. Then there are the linen closets and the staircases to the maids' rooms, and at the other end the studio. There are secret connections along all the corridors and there's the laundry chute, which I love. You can let yourself down inside it, if you know where the ledges are, and go from one floor to the next without anyone knowing. Sometimes I put things down the chute for grandpapa, or lower them down the dumb waiter. He showed me how to work the dumb waiter myself. You have to stand on tiptoes and lean in and pull on the ropes, one to make it come up and the other to let it drop. It's very secret now; hardly anyone uses it but us. We lower waste paper down it, and old squares of painted canvas. And then, when the dumb waiter has gone all the way down, I tiptoe all the way to the cellars and carry the papers to the furnace. It's exciting. It must be thick thick paper because you can hardly fold it, and if there are two sheets on top of each other you can't fold them at all. They're as stiff as cardboard and they burn well. When you slide the paper into the furnace door it lights up very brightly and you can see faces and houses and churches and girls in fancy dress, and sometimes children, and other times just lozenges and circles and squares, mostly black and white but some colours too. And some sheets of paper that are all coloured grey and silver and others that are that nice soft red colour like bricks. When they're burning well they sometimes bubble up like blisters and the shapes on the paper go all strange. After that, when I'm alone in my bed at night, I can see the shapes twisting and arching up, different from what they were when grandpapa showed them to me in the studio.

'This is your mother when she was smaller than you, my little charmer. Do you see your own face in hers? And here is the summer house at Citraguines-les-clochers, and here is the beach and the umbrellas. This is M. le Curé in his dog-cart, a good man but a poor driver of ponies. This is his pony rearing in the shafts. Poor Curé, his hat has come off. What a time that was, the surf rolling in hour after hour and the sound on the shingle to lull you to sleep. Fifty years, my little one, can you imagine what fifty years feels like in your heart? How old are you now, Fossette?'

'I will be nine on my next birthday, grandpapa.'

'A strong willing nine years old, isn't that so?'

'Oh yes, for you, yes.'

I hid from Uncle Maurice with my picture in my arms so he

wouldn't find his way to the studio door while grandpapa was busy with his task of cleaning up. He doesn't want anybody but me to know what he's doing, to save the maids work. Mamma wouldn't like it, he says, 'and poor papa would be gravely disturbed'. That's what he says, and he makes faces when he says it that are so like papa that it makes me laugh. He can imitate Uncle Maurice, you know, so that you might think they were twins.

'No, they're none of them like me, Fossette. There are none of us left, except perhaps you. Are you going to be the least and the last of the Chénonceaux? You have no brothers and sisters, only aunts and uncles and cousins. Do you like your cousins?'

'I detest them!' Grandpapa taught me to say that. It makes him laugh. I clap my hands and sing, 'Yes, I detest them, Paul and Matthew and Giles and Bettina … she looks so much like Aunt Hélène that you can't tell them apart …'

Uncle Maurice came wandering along my corridor in the shadows, calling out, looking for my room. He had a hammer in his hand, and a big picture hook. I'm sure he only wanted to help me, but the hammer looked heavy and dangerous.

'Here I am, in my cabane,' I called out.

'So I've caught you, little woman,' said Uncle Maurice. He raised the hammer to make a hole in the wall for the hook. When he'd fastened the hook into the wall and wound it tight he stood back and gazed at me. 'And that's where you'll keep it for certain?'

'Yes, uncle. Would you lift it onto the hook, please?'

He hung my picture up so that it was reflected in the mirror on the door to my armoire. I could see myself pictured twice. And if I looked in the mirror I saw my pictured face over my head and behind me.

III

Grandpapa stands in the middle of a pile of pieces of wood. 'They think I'm mad,' he tells Fossette. 'Not bad, simply mad. They don't believe that I've a right to do with my property just as I please.' He bangs on a corner of a broken stretcher with a wooden mallet, and the two pieces fly apart, the little metal corner bracket flying through the air directly into Fossette's outstretched hands. 'Good catch,' says her grandfather as she deposits the object in the correct jar. There are dozens of screw eyes, nails, corner brackets and big copper staples in the jars. Grandpapa never allows injurious metal objects to lie around on the floor. He picks them up, or Fossette picks them up and they are collected into the series of pickle jars that stand all around the studio on dusty shelves. There is a crackling noise as grandpapa presses the piece of stretcher onto the pile with his foot. Later he will bundle up the pile neatly with waxed twine and stack it with the other bundles that are lined up neatly under the eaves in the large room. The fine dried wood of the stretchers makes a serious fire hazard of which neither grandfather nor grandchild is aware. The whole studio would alarm any insurer who inspected it, gummy old tubes of paint, dozens of jars of oil, thinner, turpentine, brittle dried wood, canvas impregnated with colouring matter.

'I've no right to dispose of my property, is that what they think? Well, they'll have to reconsider the subject. These works are mine, and their only value is the marks I've made on them.'

He goes to a workbench in a shady corner and seizes a large pair of garden shears, such as are used to trim the edges of a lawn or flowerbed. He opens and shuts the shears forcibly, two or three times. They make a hissing, slicing sound like a great scissors. Then he drapes the canvas from the painting he has just taken apart across a pair of sawhorses, and stands for a moment looking at it with a hint of regret. He positions the shears at the lower right corner of the canvas and deftly cuts off the signature, done in large bold print, *DES CHENONCEAUX 1992.*

'There goes the best part of a million,' says the old man with a grim chuckle. He gazes for a moment at the unmutilated image that remains on the large canvas. 'Mathilde in a velvet gown.'

'Perhaps your mother might have liked to keep this one, but I can't allow it. I botched the job and I won't allow it to be seen. They know that anything with my signature on it is worth an enormous sum. They could have placed this mismanaged daub in a gallery and sold it to the Japanese for another million. But when I'm gone who will defend my name? The truth, my angel, the truth is that I'm past my best and I know it. Most of these things are failures.'

He kicks energetically at a sheaf of masterly drawings that lie nearby on the splintery floor. 'Trash, trash!'

He takes up the shears and cuts deeply into the awkwardly draped canvas. 'Mathilde in a velvet gown.' The gown is executed in a shining ink-green with traces of wiry gold lines snaking across its surface. 'Cloth,' snarls the old man, 'nobody tries to paint cloth now. The second-hardest subject, do you know that, Fossette? Cloth is harder to paint than almost anything else, folds and falls and shadows and gatherings.' He brings his face down almost to the child's height, and grimaces comically. Fossette giggles.

'Is there anything harder than that?'

'Only flesh. And the bones underneath.'

He points the shears at the velvet gown, where its hem appears at the ragged edge of the canvas. Then he cuts deeply into the image, opening and shutting the shears with amazing vigour for such an old man. There is a distinctive crumbling sound, like rats gnawing wood behind walls, a gobbling snapping sound. The old painter makes a cut more than a foot long at the bottom of the painting. He moves the shears further along and makes a second long cut. Then he can readily fold back the oblong formed by the half-separated piece and cut it along the top, removing a stiff, heavily painted, rectangular part of the painting and handing it to his granddaughter. It fills her arms; she holds it with familiar ease. She has held similar pieces of canvas before.

'Should I put this in the dumb waiter?'

'No, wait a bit, I'll do some more.' He works along the bottom of the ruined canvas until he has cut up and removed the entire lower quarter of the work, and with Fossette's eager help arranged the pieces in a trim stack. He spends the next hour in destroying the remainder of the large canvas in the same way. Finally he stands with his left foot on the stacked pieces of oiled and sized canvas. 'Useless,' he says, 'and they'd frame them and sell them piecemeal if they could. "Morsel of a painting I" ... "Morsel of a painting VIII". And so on until they'd disposed of all the bits and never mind my wishes. We'll fool them, my child. We'll put them in the furnace like the others. Can you manage?'

'I'll wait till they're all at dinner, grandpapa. That's the best time for secrets.'

'And do they burn easily?'

'Oh, it's exciting. They blaze up like fireworks.'

Later that evening Fossette creeps along the corridor to the dumb waiter hatchway, carrying a number of smelly squares of oil-impregnated canvas which she lowers to the cellar. What she does after that is nobody's business.

IV

'Darling, we know how much you adore your grandfather, and how he loves you in return, but really, we cannot allow you to spend all your time with him. Miss de Barny says that you are neglecting your lessons; your irregular verbs, she says, are a disgrace.'

Fossette shudders, remembering her terrible troubles over *s'asseoir* and *croître*.

'I know how to say them, mamma. I just can't write them. But I don't want to write, I want to be with grandpapa. I can help him. Sometimes he gives me a drawing lesson. He says that I may be able to do something with my drawing.'

'We never see your drawings. What becomes of them?'

'Of course we destroy them, mamma. They aren't fit to be seen. Grandpapa says that one should never allow inferior work out of the studio.'

'He says that?'

'He insists on it. He corrects all my little works and when he's covered the sheet with new lines and good advice, then I study it, and he explains where I've gone wrong, and then naturally we destroy it.'

'And that's all?'

'I beg your pardon, mamma.'

'That's all you do together, draw and confer?'

'What else should we do?'

Now her kind papa speaks in mild tones. 'You see, Fossette, your grandfather is not young any more. He seems unable to do work of his own. No doubt he feels himself to be young again, as he watches you make your little sketches. He has enough strength to correct you, but not enough to work freely on his own. He's a very old man, dear, and he needs all the help and advice his children can give him. He has not been able to do anything new for years. Now is the time for all of us in the family to club together and encourage him to mount one grand final exhibition. What we call a retrospective showing.'

'Re-tro-spec-tive?'

'That's right, child.'

'Grandpapa doesn't mean to have a re-tro-spec-tive. He told me so.' She nods her head wisely. 'He says the time for that has gone by.'

'Has he spoken to you about this?'

'Once or twice. He says he daren't sign his name to a squiggle or a doodle,' and Fossette laughs delightedly, 'sign his name to a squiggle or a doodle for fear that somebody might offer it for sale in a gallery as a late des Chénonceaux. Is that true, papa?'

'Is what true?"

'Would bad people sell grandpapa's squiggles and doodles?'

'Well, they might if they thought they could get away with it.'

'That wouldn't be a nice thing to do.'

'Out of the mouths of babes,' says papa, as the little girl leaves the room with Miss de Barny.

'Irregular verbs, darling,' says mamma. 'Be good and work hard.'

'Work hard, indeed!' says papa. 'That little mite is concealing something, *j'en suis certain*. The old man's beginning to fail; he's more and more of a recluse. He treats us as if we were his enemies.'

'But Albert, he's always been like that. He's never let any of us into his workrooms, here or at the country house or the seashore. He's always been secretive, and a slow worker.'

'He does that to manipulate his prices,' says papa with enthusiasm, 'and a superb job he's made of it. Think what he's storing up there, the work of more than a decade, canvases, drawings. The last time he admitted me – his own son – into the studio I saw that he'd begun to fashion the most exquisite little heads in clay. Think what a dozen of them would fetch. There might be enough for a show. Heads of children. Mostly little girls.'

'That is a good thing anyhow.'

'Please, my dear. There's never been any suggestion of that with him, but he's declining. He's eighty-four years old; it's only natural. And suppose his mental powers were to go suddenly, why he might do anything. He still smokes now and then. Right up there at the top of the building he might do serious damage if he were to forget something burning. I know that he makes coffee on an electric plate. Imagine what might happen if he took it into his head to heighten the scarcity value of his work by disposing of some of it. Those little clay heads could be reduced to powder in seconds. And there would go an entire show and a flood of publicity.'

'And millions.'

Albert looks at Mathilde in horror. 'There is no way to judge whether controlled scarcity would be compensated for by international demand and an extraordinary rise in evaluations.'

'I think we're faced with a potentially catastrophic situation,' says Fossette's mamma.

And indeed they are!

V

'Grandpapa, what is a catastrophic situation?'

The old man gives her a beatific smile. 'That's a very unusual period of life, child, when the very old and the very young turn the tables on the wise folk. It's a game where the powerful lose. And being unused to it, they don't like it.'

'No, I can see that they wouldn't. But why should mamma be in a catastrophic situation?'

'Does she believe that she is?'

'She says so. While we were having breakfast.'

'Poor Mathilde. What she must be suffering!'

'Suffering, grandpapa? She isn't sick, is she? Mamma is very strong, you know. I get all my strength from mamma. Look here!' Fossette doubles her right arm at the elbow and displays her plump small bicep. 'See how strong? And mamma is just like that. She can't be sick. Are we making her sick, do you think? Perhaps I shouldn't be here with you?'

'We're not making her sick, Fossette. It's an illness that only the sufferer can cause or cure. It's called greed and it does no good to the sick person or her friends, and it can only be cured by denial, either self-denial or restrictions placed on the sick by healers and jailers. Just look at your mother and father. They have everything they could possibly want, a fine home, wealth enough for anyone, a loving daughter. But they can't be satisfied with plenty, they want everything. That's the true sign of greed, dissatisfaction. What you have is never enough. You will go on and on, seeking for more goods and values, for paintings and drawings that don't exist and can never exist, but because they've been half sketched out on some imperfect surface they're accessible, they can be desired, can be transported to the sale-room in their imagined state. "It's almost finished. It's all there in the sketch. You can see what he intended even though he didn't make a success of it. Never mind that it isn't perfect, his best work, even his middling-good work. It's enough that it comes from his studio. And the public has a right to see it all, the unsigned pieces and the abandoned starts, the doodles and squiggles and the places where he went wrong."'

Grandfather begins to pace up and down the long length of the studio under the skylight. In the full midday light he has the look of some figure from the plates of William Blake, some allegory of Adam triumphing over dissatisfaction. He stares down from his great height at his small co-conspirator, almost frightening the little girl.

'God forbid that I should bring discredit on your parents in your eyes, my dear. It would be a wicked action and unworthy of an artist. They are good normal people who care for you and for themselves. They would rather die than see you in hunger or pain, but they don't understand me or my ambitions. I want to preserve my few good things and destroy all the bad. I want to allow nothing to leave here that I can't approve, no matter what the cost. I will not allow them to compromise me or to traffic in my signature. Here, you must help me, this one is too big for me to move by myself.'

It is almost the last of the large late oils, an end-of-the-millennium pastiche of the painting of the whole previous century. On a first look it appears to be a family portrait in the manner of Sargent, strongly organized along the horizontal, a work much wider than it is tall, about twelve feet wide by eight feet high, in which the rendering of the background is the principal element in the composition. Full of ancestral voices prophesying war, black and grey and indigo, smoky tones at flashpoint, a huge twilight looms over the foregrounded figures, Albert, Mathilde, Maurice and the child in the primrose summer dress. Sargent's treatment of the Sitwell family is cruelly parodied, the sumptuous clothing of the adults, the filmy gauzy dress of the child. A kitten frolics next to its basket. The carpet is an infinitely precious Shiraz reproduced in the terms of pure painting, of the use of crimsons and blues and golds that melt as we look at them into exquisite abstractions. He has called the work 'A Postmodern Family at Teatime'.

Together the old man and the child wrestle the huge object away from the wall and into the centre of the studio. They place it on the splintery floor with the painted surface uppermost. Then they walk about on the stiffly dried oil surface under their feet. The canvas crackles and splits. He takes his shears and kneels beside the sprawling splitting material at the lower right hand corner. And pierces the image of the little girl and cuts her out of the scene before attacking the rest, like somebody much younger cutting out paper dolls, the figure almost of human scale but flat and meaningless out of context and Fossette receives her excised likeness in her arms. Stands it up beside her as if to walk it about the room while her grandfather continues to cut. But her image is silent, motionless, flat.

There Are More Peasants Than Critics

All right then, picture this. An ordinary man just like us has a singular dream that persuades and entertains him in a way that his usual dreams don't. They're fragmentary, shadowy and confused, usually without suggestive power. Idle dreams. But this one, which comes to him in his mid-forties, has none of the purposeless and mocking character of other scenes out of his sleep. This one is the real goods, consecutive and bright, coloured and lighted mysteriously by an irradiation whose source is only to be guessed at. Who knows where these strong interruptions of the habitual order of our lives may originate? They come as something given, ordained elsewhere and not to be traced back.

The man's dream gradually takes on form: it's much longer than usual. He has heard like the rest of us that the time sequences that appear in our dream lives, seeming so protracted and so fully detailed, are really the creations of a few moments as we near the waking state. Can this be right, he wonders while he is dreaming the marvellous tale, can this be nothing but a signal of morning, instructions about getting up and going to the office, mere symptoms of an itchy nose or cramped toes under too heavy bedclothes? An extraordinary importance now begins to invest the story he is witnessing. He realizes strongly that this narrative is absolutely original, telling a story that he has never heard anywhere else. The story charms and delights him. Suppose that you were in the audience the first time that the parable of the prodigal son was told. Imagine hearing that tale for the first time, fresh and new and empowered with immense suggestion. From the lips and in the alluring accents of that troublesome narrator who continues to vex our imaginations. Our sleeping man knows somehow that he has arrived at a point close to the roots of narrative. The unfolding story grows more and more gripping. He has, in short, been presented with a complete work of art. It is his alone! Nobody knows this story but its solitary dreamer. Into the frame of his awareness there seeps the obvious conclusion. This is a valuable property and he knows it. He can't explain where this idea of ownership has sprung from. He isn't a professional storyteller nor any kind of artist and has no idea how these great acquisitions are brought before the public. It is something like musical creation.

In a lifetime of humming to yourself, if you are not a musician, you may come once or twice on a genuinely tasteful musical idea. You'll know when this happens because it will surprise you greatly. It's like finding a treasure in a field near the sea. You kick over a stone, really more a small boulder, and underneath it is a hoard of golden objects hidden a thousand years earlier against the maraudings of the Norsemen.

Our man is waking up. He learns the end of his magnificent discovery just at the moment that his eyes open, and the contrast between the entrancing end of his dream and the everyday appearance of his bedroom frightens him. He feels the hairs at the base of his neck stirring as though raised by an invisible presence. He rises with unaccustomed haste and goes to his trousers, slung over the back of an old armchair that leans and sags in a corner. Finds his notebook and a turquoise-coloured ballpoint pen and starts to write down his wonderful new discovery. And it is all there; he isn't forgetting it. Unlike most dream narratives, this one isn't fading quickly from memory. It seems to be extending itself as he thinks about it, and taking on new meanings. In the next few weeks our man becomes preoccupied with his beautiful, wise, inviting, revelatory parable. He sees further into it with each passing day. Although he has no talent as a writer, the power and interest of his story are so clear and distinct that they seem to equip him with enough art to get the job done.

Things like this happen; there's no doubt about it. A woman or man may witness some earthshaking event in waking life – a natural calamity or some human aberration, an earthquake or cruel act of violence, or some noteworthy human undertaking like the ascent of a high mountain – and be so moved and prompted by the sight as to find in herself an undreamt-of expressive capacity. 'I was shocked, taken right out of myself. I never saw anything like it before!' The eyewitness account of triumph or disaster has a kind of natural authenticity more convincing than photographs or filmed record. We easily read the awe, horror, exhilaration, in the untrained voice, the nervous halting episodic rendering of what has happened. The amateur voice is more convincing than the smooth, expert ordering of events provided by the professional artist.

That's how it is with our dreamer's story. Every day that passes brings new material to his attention; things concealed in his first viewing of the dream action begin to show up. Little subtleties. The wording of a half-glimpsed newspaper headline; the colours of a poster advertising some apocryphal product, say a household cleanser that doesn't exist. A national brand in a fictitious nation. He feels unable to transpose and edit, to bring out nuances that maximize the values of this gorgeous thing that has been given to him. Like a child building up a snow figure he pats fresh material onto the emerging form, first at the waist and then around the shoulders. The form of the story, its surprising sequence of events and its extraordinary climax and conclusion – at the same time surprising and wonderfully apt – all are heightened and more fully revealed as time passes and our narrator's insight into his tale deepens and chastens itself.

Now as the whole strange tool kit yields up its full meaning a challenging circumstance forces itself upon the dreamer's reflections. How can he retell the story without giving it away? Just as the parables of Christ could never have been copyrighted and put within covers to be sold as a book until their teller had gone away and the institutional church begun its life, so our man's lovely myth, once made public, would immediately transform itself into the property of the whole world. Who can possess a myth? If he even gives a hint of the beauty, power and originality of his treasure, to listeners or readers, friends or business associates, it would pass from his control and become part of the human heritage. How can he go public without sacrificing his title to it? Who owns works of art that are drawn from the common imaginative dream-stock of humanity?

He finds himself in the position of somebody who has invented a superb slogan to advertise some widely used product, a soft drink or chocolate bar, and can't see how to sell it to an advertising agency. How can you tell the secret without, as we say, giving it away? Our bewildered inventor begins to feel that he has more on his plate than he bargained for when he first dreamt his tale. They'll steal it! What is to be done?

And then, think of the difficulties of transcription: he has the elements of the story fixed in manuscript form, but he isn't certain that he has done the tale full justice. May he not be fudging the very core or nub of the narrative? Giving it a wrong emphasis while committing it to writing? Could it perhaps be an essentially oral communication? Should he try to act it out, perform it before live audiences? He suspects that communication will make its teller celebrated, even internationally celebrated. Does he want that? Should he appear in a mask, should he sign contracts under his true name? And supposing that he wins wide audience approval for the material, what can he do for an encore? One of the elements of the wonderful story that seems to him its most engaging aspect is its portrayal of a sweet and charming young woman, such a girl as makes everyone feel better about himself or herself, funny, persuasive, lovely and true. Could this human image and its emotional effect be continued and developed as the premiss for some sort of series? Is there more to the story than the story itself? He knows how it ends; that was fully delivered to him on the first morning when he woke up. He can't play around with this young woman, planting hints of possible sequels meant to milk the story of all value. He feels for the first time the author's sense of responsibility to his work. The work is never simply its author's private creation. It always comes from afar and brings demands and coercions with it. He senses that, should he somehow mess up the public embodiment of the story, he will suffer because of it. He hasn't allowed for that; at the start this gift seemed just that, something without cost that he could do with as ne pleased. But now he has second and third thoughts and worry comes behind.

Discrimination is the child of anxiety. He realizes that carrying such a gift within himself is strictly akin to pregnancy; the child must be cared for solicitously from the first moment of conception through the whole life of the parent. On her deathbed the mother thinks of her children and stretches out her hands to them, telling them not to weep for her but to be happy. In the same way the author must not only bring the conception to fruition inside her or his very self, but must defend the integrity of the work after it is brought into the world.

The dreamer has acquired debts that he doesn't know how to pay.

There is the question of audiences to consider; the reader or hearer or viewer notoriously conditions the integrity of the work. Is this wonderful narrative destined to be placed at once among the race's treasury of stories, like Christ's parables, a sophisticated work of art? Or is it a popular naive work, or can it be aimed at both sophisticated and popular readers, hearers, viewers? Our narrator has no clue to the identity of the sophisticated audience. Who are they anyway? Are they the right nurses for this child? Where can he find them? Our dreamer is an office worker in the middle way of life, not a teacher or editor or critic or poet of any kind. He guesses that his work has a double nature. Sometimes it exudes a captivating wit and subtlety that make him see it as a rather elitist production, something sly in its humour. And then again it changes into a broad, funny Falstaffian record, clearly meant for a popular audience, even a mass audience. He doesn't know which way to turn.

He has to find a consultant; somewhere in his circular round of acquaintances there must be one to whom he can entrust the substance of the story. But who? Whom? He is uncertain of the difference between who and whom, which makes him understand very clearly that he is really not competent to do justice to this vital tale that swells and rounds him out. And justice must be done to it, for now he understands that his kingly discovery is linked to his moral fate. He will be judged by the way he delivers the narrative. Whom to consult?

He has once been married but he isn't married any more, and doesn't for a moment think of calling his former wife and telling her the tale. She has another husband who might actively resent such an appeal. She would have to confide the burden of the story to her mate. He is afraid of being identified as an interfering ex-hubby, trying to make trouble. He would certainly be seen in this light. No use talking to her.

There are no children to be considered. Now he thinks about his brother, and rejects him as a confidant. This brother has made a great success of his life, in the most practical terms. He is very rich, and a kind of wisdom has been born out of his great acquisitions, not quite the wisdom required for this consultation. But he has a small daughter, a girl of twelve, Katie. And this Katie is renowned in the family and in a small circle connected with her rich parents, as an oracle or seeress. She has somehow or other gained a special peculiar insight, is one of those natural truth-tellers thrown up by human society from time to time. She is a child of immense good nature. He decides to ask Katie what she thinks. She loves fast-food outlets, so he makes an appointment for a Saturday lunch at a nearby McDonald's. The restaurant will be noisy, no chance of being overheard.

Katie orders a large fries, a bowlful of Chicken McNuggets, a shake, a cherry pie, and a quarter-pounder with cheese. Her uncle likewise orders up a lot of stuff, and they chuckle together as they carry loaded trays to the rear of the non-smoking section. There's a crowd, but as chance would have it there are a few empty tables at the back, and they are able to unload their trays without being overheard.

For a brief while there is a friendly silence as they chew their way through lunch. Katie has the most expressive eyes, and from their radiance and power of expression it is clear that she is on her top form. He asks her to give him her fullest attention. Then he tells her the story, or rather he reads his most recent transcription of it from a sizeable typescript. She listens and her shining eyes grow big and round as he goes along. When he gets down to the last bits, which include some sparkling dialogue between the main personages of the story, Katie starts to wriggle in her chair with enjoyment and the urge to frame some comments on what she is hearing. When he reaches the ending she can't hold back any longer. 'Where did you hear that?'

'I made it up.'

'Uncle, you never did! Why, it's marvellous, fantastic, uncanny. It's really really good.'

'You like it?'

'I love it. Are you going to publish it?'

She takes his authorship absolutely for granted, which pleases him more than he can say. 'Actually, I dreamt it, so I guess it belongs to me. I intend to publish it, but where, Katie? Any suggestions? Would it be a popular success or should I aim at the critics?'

She looks straight at him and her eyes darken with thought. He feels a pang of compunction at having troubled this little girl with his problem, but he is underestimating his niece. For a moment she glances away and chases a final Chicken McNugget around her plate, grasps it thoughtfully and pops it into her mouth. There is a crunching noise; she swallows, pauses, then speaks.

'Well, uncle, it always seems to me that there are more peasants than critics.'

And of course there are.

The uncle finds this utterance strongly persuasive, even compelling, gnomic. It has the authenticity of the truly evangelical.

'Will you have something more to eat?' he asks. He has the impulse to reward her richly, and understands as the impulse fills him how he has not become as rich as his brother, who has gifts that are like Katie's, and at the same time not like Katie's. The apple doesn't fall far from the tree. But it does fall some small distance away. What has been a finely honed acquisitive instinct in his brother has been transformed in this child to a generalized understanding of motive.

'I'll have another pie, apple this time if you don't mind.'

'Drink your shake,' he says, 'and I'll go get your pie.' He can feel her eyeing him as he makes his way to the counter. 'Sir,' says a young man at the counter, 'I forgot to tell you before that you can buy a Bugs or Daffy doll for sixty-nine cents with any order over four ninety-five. Do you want one now?'

He buys a Daffy Duck doll for Katie as well as her pie.

'For me? How lovely! I'll think of him as my uncle's Daffy. My uncle the author.' She finishes the pie, bundles her trash onto a tray and into the disposal bin, and accompanies her uncle to the parking lot. It is clear from her behaviour as he drives her home that she won't betray his confidence. He doesn't have to ask her not to tell his story to anybody, and especially not to her father. If her dad were to hear about it prior to publication, Time/Warner would at once appear and offer its possessor all the kingdoms of the earth for first rights.

He drops Katie off at the family condo, smiles at her with deep gratitude and turns for home. There he seats himself immediately at his keyboard and starts to type out the last and definitive version of the story that you are now about to read ...

How Did She Find Out?

Poisoning is a woman's crime.

– Andersen, *Lore and Language of Crime Fiction*

Could there be anything to that, he asked himself. Few women are physically strong enough to beat a man to death, and obtaining the murder weapon, knife, bludgeon or firearm, must always pose an inconvenient consideration to a woman. Some question of gender dignity surfaces at once when the purchase of a handgun or switchblade is at issue. Poison seems more conveniently acquired. Classical excuses for its purchase can be fabricated after a casual examination of the literature of murder; unblocking stopped sinks, putting down wasps' nests, other routine chores, may necessitate the purchase of one of the cyanides or of a corrosive hydroxyl. A decent woman need feel no embarrassment at asking for Plumber's Helper or Drano in the hardware store. A dollop of these tangy crystals in the soup and Bob's your uncle. Maybe it really is a woman's crime, he thought, revolving the question persistently in quiet moments.

He had never before been subject to sudden shifts in his state of health, but ever since his last birthday there had been peculiar incidents in his health history. Unpredictable nausea, sudden agonizing headaches. The strange matter of the blue birthday cake. His last birthday cake, when he'd turned sixty-four, had really been blue, enrobed in a thick gooey creamy icing of a tint he'd been warned off as a child. There are no non-toxic blue colourings, they had told him when as an infant he had licked blue paint from his crib. Was that a grandmother's tale, or were all blues fatal if consumers licked them up? He didn't know, but the cake had had a threatening look. He had eaten two thick slices topped with fancy ice cream that masked the flavour of the icing; it had been smooth and cold but unidentifiable as an arsenate. His headaches had begun a day or two after the party.

They might be an expression of the aging process. Maybe all the new sensations that invaded his body space over the following months were the natural accompaniments of advancing years. Perhaps. But as he catalogued them the dozens of Sayerses and Christies and Allinghams, consumed light-heartedly as recreation, began to trickle back into his consciousness. Taken together they gave weight to menace, to suspicion. Obscure muscular aches and spasms. What caused them? Sudden twitchings of the muscles and joints in bed at night. Too heavy bedclothes? Too much jogging? Or strychnine? Where could she obtain strychnine, and how administer it? He seemed to remember that it could be prepared from a decoction of some wildflower. Was it foxglove? Thinking on this subject was impaired by the fact that he wouldn't have recognized foxglove if she'd been growing it in window boxes on the condo sills. Was it a small bluish flower, source of some of the blue tints against which he'd been warned? If you lick the paint on your crib you'll get strychnine poisoning!

Unfamiliar stomach pains that came and went at intervals of say two months, followed by suspiciously copious bowel movements about which he was reluctant to speak to anybody! You can't make inquiries of this kind to the family doctor who has known both of you for forty years. Suppose you're wrong about this! Think how the doctor will judge you for harbouring such idiotic guesses. Come to that, he'd known her first, and would be on her side. The husband would come out looking very bad, cruel, neurotic, anxiety-ridden. What possible motive could he have ... etc., etc.

Motive, means, opportunity, he recalled, were the holy trinity of reflections about murder. He remembered that present-day forensics tended to play down motive as the leading element of criminal investigation. Means to hand and a chance to isolate your target were far more important than reasons for wishing him or her dead. A chance to kill, and a big rock handy, or a decoction from foxglove, there you are! Perhaps she didn't need a motive; the whole procedure might spring from whim.

He was not a rich man. She could have very little to gain by putting him out of the way; yet the disturbing symptoms persisted, and came more frequently as the year wore on. He held a responsible executive post close to the top of a multinational. While he had never had any capital, there were salary and savings. He earned about a hundred and twenty-five thousand annually, and current earnings would stop when he did. Surely that would shield him from whim or impulse. Sometimes when they met over the breakfast table he imagined that her eyes glittered and her smile merged into a grimace. The house was already in her name. He must be imagining this, and really ought to see somebody about these neurotic insecurities.

It occurred to him to cast up his net worth, simply to make certain that financial gain could form no part of her calculations. He passed some evenings overhauling his records, salary cheque stubs, bankbooks. Suddenly a fact struck him that might provide a clue. His company paid for a group insurance policy for senior executives that was designed as an estate-builder in the event of early death. It had a large face value to age sixty-five, then the cash yield declined sharply with every subsequent passing birthday.

He'd completely forgotten about this.

Until his sixty-fifth birthday, according to the insurer's brochure, the policy paid a lump sum at death equal to four times the value of annual salary, in his own case a payoff of five hundred thousand! Afterwards the sum payable declined with each passing birthday: one hundred thousand until you were sixty-six; seventy-five thousand until sixty-seven; fifty thousand until sixty-eight; twenty-five thousand until sixty-nine. After that the face value levelled off at ten thousand and remained there until insured's decease, paying just enough to get you decently underground.

Certainly it was generous of his employers to provide this coverage. How would the taxing authorities treat payment to beneficiary? Would the whole amount be subject to tax or would the bereaved be free of such punitive taxation? He kept in his study with his records some fat volumes on estate law and levy. From a careful perusal of a handbook devoted to these matters he learned that, subject to certain exceptions that would not apply in her case, the beneficiary would receive the whole sum untaxed, half a million. And neither of them had ever been able to lay their hands on a capital sum. Say what you like, half a million is still to be considered as a capital sum, and a fairly substantial one at that. It amounted to this: he was worth half a million on the hoof until midnight on the last day of his sixty-fifth year. On the stroke of midnight his cash surrender value – as he rather grimly put it to himself – dropped to one-fifth of what it had been the moment before. This was apart from certain other provisions for inheritance, pension rights, small bank accounts, and so on.

The provisions of the group policy amounted, he saw, to provocation, even to incitement. Such inducements to beneficiaries were tactless at least, and possibly a sufficient motive for resort to the alleged 'woman's crime', slow poisoning. Such arrangements ought not to be tolerated. If they wanted to be generous to employees, why not shower them with less risky benefits? Paid vacations at luxury resorts, free medical care, things that a couple might enjoy jointly without either of them being moved to dispose of the other, so as to enjoy the benefits alone. But five hundred thousand dollars? He was worth much more dead than alive.

Wry thoughts of insurances and insurance scams began to trouble him. Did anybody ever contrive his or her own death to take advantage of the foolish provisions of group policies like this? Why did the insurers do such things anyway? The answer was clear: the companies have access to the best actuarial services in the world. They know that very few executives die before sixty-five. Most of the pampered occupants of the executive suites, free from worry about their finances even in recessionary times, live on past the date when the large amount is due. Group insurers know what's what. Nobody cheats them. You have to live almost forever to beat them on an annuity. People in his group lived at least into their early seventies, when the insurer would see them decently buried and no hard feelings. But until the bell of midnight tolled a few months in the future, his life, in one sense at least, wasn't worth a plugged nickel. It was his death that was valuable; he had no intention of abridging his life-span to beat the actuaries.

He sat in his study surrounded by group insurance forms, pension records, the detritus of forty years of a working lifetime. It seemed to him that some of the material was not in its customary order, that the creases in the insurance policies were folded the wrong way, so that the thick documents didn't slide into their plastic envelopes as easily as usual. Had his papers been tampered with?

How did she find out? He pulled a single strand of hair from the back of his neck, where his hair grew thickest and longest, retaining some of its original chestnut colour, and laid the hair carefully along some of the folds in the bulky policy. Then he reinserted the folded paper in its envelope, meaning to check its position at some time well before his next birthday. If the hair was missing or disarranged he would know that somebody was up to something. *Does she know for certain?* With a cool half-million, ownership of the house free and clear, the pension payments, the car and the rest of their stuff, she'd be a moderately rich woman.

He must be very careful. His suspicions had been aroused at first by that series of sharp sickening headaches, which now, with some months remaining before the crucial date, were replaced by equally troublesome stomach pains, followed in their turn by acute muscular and joint discomforts in the upper body, accompanied by dizziness. He now began to observe her very closely and to take great pains not to eat anything in the least questionable. He checked his documents once or twice to see if the brown hair in the policy had been disarranged; once it seemed as though it might have been disarranged but he couldn't be certain about that. Was she checking his papers when he was out of the house? He had never kept them under lock and key. To do so now would alert her to his awareness of her presumably guilty purposes. Had she gone through his things? Had she really found out or was he imagining all this?

Most nights now he spent in reviewing his Agatha Christies, looking for the symptoms of poisoning. This prolific author, he recalled, had passed much of the First World War on duty in the pharmacy of a large hospital. There she had acquired some real knowledge of the standard toxicology, the kinds of poisons, their effects, their detectibility. The smell of bitter almonds, the metallic taste on the back of the tongue.

A metallic taste; what did that indicate? Wasn't it arsenic, administered as one of its salts? Whitish-brown powder readily soluble in liquids, tea, coffee, soup. He thumbed through several Sayers and Christie books and learned some curious facts. In one of these mischievous fictions the killer had cunningly taken advantage of the fact that it is possible to habituate yourself to arsenic consumption, so as to become practically immune to its effects. You could then partake of the same food as your victim who, unused to the poison, would succumb at once while you showed no ill effects and went free of suspicion. Could she be pulling such a stunt, nibbling away at a poison to immunize herself, while preparing for the frontal assault on his digestive tract?

If so, there was little to be gained by insisting that they eat from the same dishes and that she go first ... but some obscure need made him wait at every meal until she began to eat her share of the dish. Now and then he thought that he caught her looking at him over her napkin or fork with alarming attention. Watching for the start of an attack? And what was a metallic taste anyway? Metallic? Naggingly chilly? Burning? It is almost impossible, he realized, to describe a taste sensation. And he dredged up from some almost forgotten course in introductory psychology the notion that there were only four basic tastes, sweet, sour, what were the other two? He could not remember but metallic wasn't one of them. Confusion. Fear.

His confusions became heavily entangled when he remembered – according to his elementary psychology textbook – that our taste sensations are mostly derived from and intermingled with smell. If you hold your nose while drinking coffee, the pleasant flavour almost completely vanishes. It is the aroma of freshly brewed coffee that determines the taste we mistakenly suppose unmediated by odour.

On this view it would be idle to try to detect the presence of a poison in food or drink – which might be why so many poisoners got away with their covert actions for a while. The victim doesn't identify the toxic substance, is unaware of its presence. Who can say what a taste tastes like? Or whether it is an unmixed taste? Poison given before breakfast would certainly be masked by the flavour of 'jungle mouth' or overnight bad breath. He knew that anything he tasted before his excited tooth-scourings and orange juice (he also brushed his tongue compulsively) struck him as poisonous in flavour. She could have given him anything at all before 8:00 a.m. and he'd never have suspected a thing.

He asked her to switch from large boxes of breakfast cereal to those small individually-wrapped packages, and refused to take the puffed rice or fruit loops from any but a freshly-opened box. He thought this puzzled and confused her. Did she realize that he was on to her? Was he on to her, or was the whole thing baseless and an insult to a loyal life companion?

Time was passing; the stomach aches and muscle kinks began about ten weeks before he was to turn sixty-five. If he were allowed to survive until then he might justly conclude that the whole tissue of suspicions was entirely of his own manufacture. He would be glad to learn this, and at the same time deeply ashamed of his surreptitious mistrust. Fair enough, he'd accept that burden if the time to take it ever came. He would willingly exchange a moderate amount of self-hatred for survival into the late sixties. Anybody would; at that price it was a bargain.

Meanwhile phrases like 'Let's eat out together for a change', and 'I'll just zap something in the microwave', surfaced more and more often in his chats with her. Dinners were the tricky times. He got his lunch at the office, where she couldn't follow him (unless she had an accomplice who was accompanying him to lunch … but no …), and breakfast was no problem. He divided his orange into halves himself. Clearly the object hadn't been tampered with (unless she was penetrating it with a syringe … no, that's crazy …). He gave up toast, the fresh fruit was enough. He could grab a decaf at the machine in the office. Dinner was dodgy. Then he exercised maximum caution, waiting for her to start, watching while she opened a package of ice-cream or some other frozen object to which nothing could have been added, diet TV dinners, lasagnas.

It struck him that she flushed with pleasure a few times when he asked her out to dine. Or was that the angry flush of frustration? You couldn't tell. She looked friendlier when she had a high colour, but then she always had. His birthday was due in a very few nights. Midnight of the twenty-fourth would tell the story. Hang on, buddy, he thought, be shrewd, be cagey, outsmart her. He checked the position of the hair in the document three or four times in the last days, but could detect no movement. Ask her out to dine on the final night. Placate her!

Last evening together, Al Dente at eight. Mineral water from an untouched bottle. A nice Orvieto that the waiter opened for them.

Pasta that her hands had never touched. Espresso. But surely the espresso was awfully bitter. He squeezed his nose shut as his wife stared, and sampled his espresso again. The bitterness vanished. The waiter hovered.

'Did I make it too strong, sir? I know you always like it strong.'

He gasped with relief. 'It's just right,' he said, and he sipped gingerly at the remaining half-cup. 'I'll take another,' he told the waiter.

His wife remonstrated with him. 'You know it'll keep you awake.'

'Ah, but I want to be up at midnight.'

'You need your rest,' she said, 'birthday boy.' But she sat on with him through the second espresso, another bottle of Orvieto, the comfortable, idle, after-dinner chat. They strolled home together, only a few blocks. Idling, window-shopping, stopping to tie a shoelace, just teasing her, he got them home just at midnight. As they came in the front door he glanced at his watch and saw that the hour of twelve had come and gone. He'd imagined the whole thing. He'd make it up to her. He'd apologize humbly for his neurotic fantasies.

But should he? In the morning it struck him that of course she'd be afraid to go for the half million, too big a payoff, and she'd be a prime suspect. But a hundred thousand? Wouldn't excite attention. Would she do it for a hundred thousand? For seventy-five? We are never free from the need to suspect, he thought, nor of the weight of suspicion.

Finishing Together

(For Terry Edwards)

I

Harold Lacey, violin, Sylvia Warshow, cello, and Nella McBride, piano, joined forces fresh out of music school six years ago to form the Warshow Trio. They chose Sylvia's surname to identify the group, not because she was their star performer nor because of her looks onstage, which were striking but no more than those of her fellow performers. She had vaguely eastern-European features, but no specially Slavic fire or zest. She was an accomplished player with affectionate manners and a full round tone that suited their ensemble. They used her name because it had a European flavour, somewhat like that of other celebrated chamber groups, the Budapest, the Amadeus, the Borodin ... the Warshow. Why not? And her given name had pleasantly literary and even classical associations. They became the Warshow Trio at graduation, and at once began to acquire a reputation as the most promising of the younger chamber groups. They were said to possess a remarkable quality of balance and reciprocal rapport, a certain something that marks out the really great chamber music ensembles, that ability to foresee sudden departures from rehearsed norms and to make adjustments in the middle of a performance, which can't be taught by the finest of coaches.

There is something to the idea that great chamber music groups are born, not made. Harold, Sylvia and Nella complemented and balanced each other so finely, as they developed their repertoire, that they seemed almost like brother and sisters. There was a family feeling to their sound that audiences responded to at once. For a while they almost began to resemble one another in appearance, like loving siblings. This quality stole into their playing, especially in the great monuments of the literature for piano trio: the two Schubert trios, the 'Archduke', the Ravel, the last dozen by Joseph Haydn.

They combined sweetness with strength in their sound; it was impossible for the critics of the daily papers in the towns they visited to pick out one of the three as their musical leader.

In a piano trio the violinist may look like the director because of the prominence of the position the player takes onstage, and the penetrating tone of the instrument. The pianist might naturally receive the next degree of attention, the percussive qualities of the instrument and the immense volume of sound produced by the modern concert grand ensuring a share of the audience's focus. This seems to assign a less prominent role to the cellist, but the players in the Warshow Trio proved as time went on to be wisely respectful of the sound of the quiet instrument; they were careful to let it through in ensemble passages. Even in the wonderful late trios of Haydn, where the writing for cello seems understated and perhaps a little out of balance, the slenderness of the cello parts was fully allowed for by Harold and Nella in their natural devotion to an ideal sound balance. You could always hear the terse ingenious writing for the cello in their Haydn pieces, whose grave beauty, far from lapsing into routine, frequently showed the stately, hymnodic movement of other late-Haydn pieces. For a while the group considered making the late-Haydn trios their speciality. But then they decided that these subtle compositions weren't quite what was wanted to build their performance reputation. They continued to use them as curtain-raisers, occasionally scheduling an all-Haydn program. Their sweet and subtle sound continued to be based upon the qualities of motivic invention and surprising key-relationship typical of the composer. If there is a Haydnish sound in chamber music, they had it. Even the critics saw it.

II

Critics and reviewers, goodness yes! In papers like the North Battleford *Examiner* and the Churchill *Journal*, the Lethbridge *Plainsman*, the Yellowknife *Miner*. Oh, how they toured in their first years, crisscrossing the continent on the university-concert-hall and civic-arts-centre circuit, often by rail, sometimes by air, mostly on buses that ran far into the north, up highways that turned into mere secondary roads, more gravel than blacktop, sometimes more mud than gravel. They loved the work, developed an enormous repertoire, learned how to examine new scores under the dim lighting provided by the electrical system of a bus. Later on Harold found that he had come to associate certain classics of the trio literature with that unique odour of exhaust fumes and worn rubber that pervades the rear seats of buses down by the toilet, the only spot where the three of them could sit side by side.

The brief Opus 87 of Brahms, first studied by the little group on a bumpy back road somewhere north of Prince Albert, Saskatchewan, became linked in the violinist's imagination with a dotted rhythm originating somewhere in the bus's tires and wheels, an insidious bump, bump, bumpety-bump, that crept into his store of musical imagery and then into performance. The women would complain that Harold's tempi sounded vehicular, roadbound. They were only teasing him; at the same time he used to find himself thinking of Brahms when on a bumpy bus, or of buses when deep into Brahms on the concert stage.

He remembered admiring Sylvia's back and shoulders, curved over the shrouded cased cello, as she humped her instrument along the narrow aisle from the rear seat to the exit, somewhere in the Peace River country. He reckoned that Sylvia had toted her instrument on and off a hundred and seventy-six buses in their first three years of touring. Often he was called upon to assist her, a circumstance that sometimes troubled him. There was the distinct inconvenience to be dealt with; it wasn't his cello, and after all he had his violin to look out for. The violin was every bit as fine an instrument as her cello. They were creations of the Italian eighteenth century, on loan to the group from the Conservatory collection, through the good offices of the cultural agency that arranged and supervised their travels.

'This concert has been funded by the National Council for the Musical Performing Arts. Mr Lacey's violin, the celebrated Amalfi "Angelica" of 1745, has been loaned to him through the sponsorship of NCMPA.' Sometimes Harold felt that he and the two young women were on loan to themselves under council sponsorship. He was the custodian of the celebrated 'Angelica' while at the same time assisting Sylvia with her precious freight. He began to precede her along the aisle, then step down from the front exit and take the case from her anxious arms, lowering it with reverence to the ground while Nella hung on to his violin case. They enjoyed helping each other in those days; it seemed to reflect their ideal of performance. Nothing terrible ever happened to either instrument. When you play a violin that is worth more than all your other possessions put together, you tend to idolize it. One of the elements in their group relations was this profound respect for the celebrated violin and cello, plus a certain disrespect for the pianos encountered on their northerly excursions. Heintzman of Toronto, said the lettering over the keyboard as often as not, or possibly Mason and Risch. Steinways they weren't. Rowboat-shaped, varnished deep black, ancient, these pianos loomed in the lives of the citizenry as their chief links to metropolitan art and culture; they were invariably present to welcome the musicians to the arts centre or high-school auditorium where they were to perform that night.

At least, thought Harold, I don't have to wrestle that monster off the bus and push it uptown. Thank God! The pianos might have slippery keys, might be indifferently tuned at best, might have unresponsive actions, but they didn't have to be carried on and off the bus. This was something to be valued.

If they had arrived in town early enough they would make their way to the auditorium in late afternoon for an hour's rehearsal, mostly to allow poor Nella to find her way around the defects of the piano, the sticking keys, the slack *una corda,* so as to help her to conceal them in that evening's performance. They used to try and persuade the local authorities to have a tuner on hand for some fast work at intermission; the second half of the concert often sounded better than the first; they learned to program the more demanding works at the beginning of the second half when the piano was freshly tuned. Afterwards they would tell people that they had acquired their true professionalism during those years of coping with the uncertain sonorities of local pianos. They certainly matured artistically on those buses and in the parish halls.

Their personal relations matured too. Three people can hardly work together in conditions of revealing intimacy for several years without their affections becoming aroused and skewed in one or another direction. A man and two women, on tour together, bound by close ties of artistic understanding, must finally determine which of them is to take the lead in the group, which two are the backup. For a long time it seemed to Harold that he as the violinist should direct their rehearsals and choose most of the works they added to their repertoire, and have most to say about choice of tempo and the nuances of performance. At piano trio performances, audiences naturally seem to offer most of their attention to the violinist, because the violin sound is more immediately audible than that of the cello. And in most cases he gives the signal for the players to begin, a trickier matter than it seems. Composers for these instruments sometimes make it easy for the performers to get started by beginning the piece with a solo passage, the others joining in at indicated bars, but this is an obvious ploy. The public likes to hear the trio start simultaneously; it is a small musical feat they consider their due. Artists have to pay some serious attention to this matter of starting together. Finishing together is even more worrisome and more problematic. Any trio can learn to start together. Finishing successively, especially in slow tempos, can expose ineptitude in a chamber group. The closing bar comes out ragged and the players seem awkward and harassed.

III

Maybe giving the upbeat all the time is unhealthy food for the ego. Given the lie of most piano-trio scores, the violinist gives the upbeat and the trio begins to play on the downbeat, all three sounding together in the striking differences of tone that make this form of chamber music so attractive. The top line of the music belongs by right to the violinist, but a skilful composer can vary the presentation of the outer voices in innumerable ways: by silencing the violin and allowing the cello to soar into its upper register, or by giving the pianist long solo passages or by handing phrases from a broken melodic line to each player successively. The form rivals the string quartet in the challenges it offers to musical invention. The percussive keyboard sound, balanced against the two stringed instruments, causes the most interesting of these problems. In the Warshow Trio, the keyboard player was a woman, the cellist another woman, but the violinist was male, and he got to give the upbeat most of the time. After some years of this Harold naturally felt pretty bossy. It might be called the Warshow Trio but it was really his group. He began to give little flourishes with his bow, as they got ready to play, little shifts in his chair, shufflings, a lean forward to adjust the score on the music stand, devices that were at first unconscious; later they became self-conscious, and caused mutterings from the other members of the group. He thought of playing from a standing position, claiming that his legs cramped up while he sat, especially in longer works. It would be better if he could move around a bit in the Schubert Op. 99.

'I have to stay sitting down,' said Sylvia touchily. This was the first serious – perhaps not so very serious – difference that they'd ever encountered. 'My bum and my thighs get all sweaty, but you don't hear me complaining.' She looked over at Nella, obviously expecting support from the other woman. Two against one, she thought.

'I don't think many trios have the violinist on his feet,' said Nella hesitantly.

Harold dismissed the remark. He said, 'I don't doubt that somewhere in this world there's a trio with an erect violinist.' The phrasing just popped out. 'Besides, I can give a more readable upbeat when I'm on my feet. Let's give it a try.'

So they tried it for a couple of rehearsals, but it didn't work out. The women complained that Harold was jigging around in a perpetual dancing commentary on the music, like a jazz violinist; they found this unsettling. He gave up the proposal, which had never been a crucial matter with him anyway; he had really floated it to find out what his status with the women was. For by now, four or five years into their association, it was clear to him that they half expected him to fall in love with one of them. His choice would drastically affect their professional lives, so he hesitated a long while before trying to decode his feelings. He wasn't a physically passionate man; most of his emotional vitality went into the music. But he felt that he should make a commitment, probably to the pianist. He didn't feel the same rivalry towards Nella that he did with Sylvia, his fellow string player. Violinists and cellists always get along with difficulty, in a recurrent competitive spirit that goes all the way back to the beginnings of ensemble performance and *ars antiqua*. The cello has a deeper and more romantic sound, but it can't produce the nimble and penetrating tones of the violin. The two instruments form a natural metaphor for the gender relationship. In the present case the woman held the deep-toned instrument, and the man the soprano voice. This was probably not very significant, in the relations between Harold and Sylvia.

He could readily have fallen in love with her even though she belonged to the cello party (where are viola players located in this competition?). But there was the solid reality of that darned old cello. He was a patient man, he got along fine with both women, but there was always the cello to be lugged on and off the bus. He'd be married to the cello as much as to its player!

It might seem far-fetched to suppose that a little thing like this could influence a man's emotional set to the extent that he would fall in love with somebody because he didn't have to carry her instrument. But who can appreciate the effects of the slow accretion of resentment in the human heart, produced by years of repeated minor inconvenience? Harold inclined to prefer Nella as a companion for several reasons, but the omnipresent cello certainly affected the choice.

The ever-varying power relationships among members of chamber-music groups are always troublesome; everybody in music performance can give examples of quartets and trios and duos whose members have been at each other's throats for years. A quartet may come into existence and win a great reputation, with its personnel unchanged for a decade. Then the viola player gives notice that she just can't take the crap any more. She might as well be playing the second viola parts in the Mozart quintets. Nothing to do, no notice from anybody, no voice in selection of repertoire. Off she goes! They find another viola player, this time choosing a man (not so flighty, they think, more stable) and find that his dark-velvet richness of sound alters the whole balance of the ensemble. Either they have to get rid of their new violist, or replace the cellist, or rethink their whole conception of balance, or make some other drastic modification of their performance attitudes. Legends exist of groups that have earned international celebrity while all four members hated one another with passionate vigour, even while two of them were husband and wife, and a third the husband's brother.

In that famous case, the husband's brother ran off to South America with the wife, where they went into business as a violin/viola duo. The experiment failed because of the slenderness of the repertoire. They had some transcriptions made but it didn't help; eventually they undertook separate solo careers where they are still trying to get started, on different continents.

The Warshow Trio wasn't in quite that state, but they did have their little problems. Harold found himself hitching around in his chair to watch Nella at the keys. A timid woman, he thought, but a superb musician: quite a combination of qualities.

IV

They used to book themselves into adjoining rooms in motels. The women took the double and Harold might have a smaller room next door, with a communicating door. The management now and then made faces about unlocking the communicating door, as though the trio – serious musicians – might be getting up to some odious sexual romp. This was not so. They wanted the door open so that they could confer freely about that night's concert program. It's amazing how effective group discussion can be when you're trying to edit your tempi. The Warshow Trio was making its name because of its fluidity in performance, which owed a lot to these late-afternoon consultations in various motels. It never occurred to any of the three to ask that the door be fastened shut for the sake of privacy, until in the fifth year of their association Harold began to find the door closed and even bolted when they arrived back in their rooms after the concert. This puzzled him. The door had been open at 5:30. Why should it be shut now?

He rarely knocked at the closed door, but did now and then stand beside it in the late evenings, tired from the energy output of the performance, to hear what he could hear. Lately he'd observed a few minor adjustments in their voicing. He might, for example, have the sense that he was being treated like the soloist in some big concerto, while Nella and Sylvia provided a supporting orchestral sound. This isolated him, while turning them into a co-operative cello and piano duo.

He wondered whether there was much repertoire for cello and piano.

He never heard snuggling sounds or gigglings aimed at excluding him from some love relationship. They were as friendly in the morning as they had always been. They weren't necessarily sleeping together, but they might be. Harold was ashamed when he had thoughts like these. He worried that any such shift in their attitudes to one another might get into their playing, the most precious element in the relationship. For they were not a set of three highly individualized performers, who worked together for convenience, not for the sake of the music. They were three integrally related musicians whose talents united to form a single entity, no member of which was more important than the others. Harold insisted on this principle whenever he stationed himself on his bedside to stare at the flat surface of the closed communicating door.

Sometimes he could hear them humming together, or strong feet, probably Nella's feet, tapping out the rhythms of some trio movement they were working up for performance. Once, to comfort himself, he took up the tapping rhythm on the closed door, to let them know he could hear what was going on. Then the tapping from the adjoining room stopped abruptly. Nella's feet, though elegantly shaped and prettily coloured, were sizeable. She was considered by the others to be sensitive on that score. Perhaps she wouldn't mind Sylvia seeing them bare, but she had never exposed them to Harold's inspection. After a series of minor incidents of this type, Harold began to see where he was. The girls had not been waiting for him to choose between them; they were simply in love with each other.

Not long after he realized this, he started to notice that when he gave an upbeat they responded like a duo, with accompanying violin obbligato. This was a hard cross to bear, as any experienced player of chamber music will tell you. Now the group sound began to move in a surprising direction. They weren't playing like a trio any more, nor like a violin soloist and a little orchestra. They were reversing the entire chamber-music tradition, in which the leading violinist sits on top of the music. Now these cunning women were making the dark, haunting lower half of the music the principal element in their interpretations. This made the literature for piano trio completely different, revised almost out of critical recognition. If the Warshow Trio had not visited Saskatoon, say, or Winnipeg, for a year or two, the critics made a point of mentioning how exotic and darkly hued their sound had become.

> In this radical reappraisal of the trio repertoire, the Warshow Trio takes the lead among North American performers, playing in a style more reminiscent of contemporary Russian ensembles, percussive, tempestuous, shadowy.
> – Barnes: *Free Press*

> Powerful, dominated by female musicality.
> – Hodinott: *Leader-Post*

This shift in stance has helped to propel the trio towards its enormous recent successes. Nowadays the buses and the secondary roads are far behind them. CBC FM courts them for dates. Recording companies keep knocking on their doors. Argo, Dorian, Waterbird, Next Century. They've recently issued their fifth CD, a runaway success. Brahms and Schumann sounding like somebody pouring melted chocolate out of a fine ceramic jug. Not your idea of Brahms? Well, perhaps not, but the reception of the record shows that lots of listeners go for chocolate Brahms, Schumann cocoa.

They only quarrelled openly once, when Nella and Sylvia finally came to feel that they must reveal the truth about their love to their associate. They invited him to their room one night in March of this year, in the Royal York in Toronto, a hotel very handy to the new CBC headquarters. Arms twining around each other's waists, cheeks close, they had to admit to Harold that they'd been thinking of breaking away as the Warshow/McBride Duo, cello and piano.

'But you can't do that,' Harold gasped. 'There's no repertoire.'

'There's the big Rachmaninoff,' said Nella brightly, thinking of the piano part, 'and the Elliot Carter.'

Had they been working up the literature under cover?

'And there's always the Brahms,' said Sylvia.

Harold began to beg them not to do this, and in the end he talked them around at least for the moment. They continue to astound audiences with their maturity and with a quality to their playing that was certainly never there before. Less Haydnish and more Shostakovichian. There's a hard taut edge to their playing, a nervous intensity, that seems a good sound for these times.

Pain Control

Suddenly everybody's a physiotherapist! Six months ago I'd never heard of ibuprofen; now they're advertising it on TV under a lot of different brand names, and you don't need a prescription, you just pick up Advil or Motrin off the shelves in the pain-control wing of the pharmacy, that long colourful stretch of shelving with the hundreds and hundreds of little boxes, and bottles. Medication.

'I hate my medication.'

'I've got to be very careful I don't forget to take my medication.'

'She went off her medication and now look what's happened.'

Megan and I went down to visit one of her girlfriends in the Neuro. I don't have to spend much time in hospitals yet, but I thought we ought to go. Nobody else from the health-food store turned up. I've noticed that the health-food people tend to stay away from hospitals. Why do you suppose that is? Competition between two health-care systems? Ethical conflict? What is the opposite of 'holistic'? You know, holistic medicine and that. I asked Vernon but he just made fun of me, like guys do.

'Stéphanie, don't worry about it. In a hundred years we'll all be dead.'

'I can't help wondering,' I said. You'd think I didn't have a full bundle of sticks.

'"Partistic"?' he said, making a joke of it. God, the remarks they come up with. Anyway we went down to visit Flo in the Neuro; she was in for a CT scan and some tests, just an overnight stop. She had to go back later for the procedure.

We got into the wrong lot; we made an illegal left turn and crossed the yellow line. Megan was driving. Later she got a ticket for it in the mail. The ticket was for thirty-five dollars! What you get for going to the hospital to see a good friend. Flo is doing fine, by the way, and making a good recovery.

On the way back to the parking lot we took a shortcut through the Royal Vic. We went up the stairs and along a sort of enclosed bridge that brought us out on the third floor of the Vic. From there is only a short walk to the lot, if you could find it, that is. We wandered around for a while, just satisfying our curiosity. Nobody asked us to show ID. Finally – still on the third floor – we found ourselves passing a wide-open doorway over which in big letters in bright red paint it said PHYSIOTHERAPY. We peeked in. There were five or six men and women sitting along a bare, ugly table, doing different things with their heads and arms, stretches, very slow. They had small pieces of equipment, which looked like fun to play with, toys for adults. Further back in the room, other people were lying flat on uncomfortable-looking mats. A tall blonde woman, younger than us, was standing between us and her patients, but not in any attempt at concealment. She seemed cheerful and interested in everything they were doing.

'Come on, Wally!' she said. 'Dig that thumb down into the theraplast. It won't bite you.' Wally grimaced.

'Very tacky,' he said in a determined voice. I thought that was brave of him. They were having serious fun, if you see what I mean. There was a wide white table on little wheels outside a glassed-in cubicle, probably the physiotherapist's office. There were some interesting objects on the table: different-sized weights, balls of various kinds and sizes, and a set of those V-shaped grippers that you use to test the strength of your hands and fingers. I don't know what to call them exactly. You can buy them in any good sports-equipment outlet.

The collection of hand weights interested me. I could imagine all the movements you could make with them, to tone your arms and shoulders. They had lots of those doughnut-shaped rings, soft, like beanbags, floppy but not completely shapeless. They seemed to come in pairs, according to a colour code. The smallest ones, one-pound weights, were covered in a shiny silky blue material; the hole was just wide and stretchy enough to take your fingers, while gripping the weight with your thumb. Starter weights, I thought. I didn't see any that looked smaller than a pound.

While we stood in the doorway peeking in, one of the male patients came up to the physio and whispered to her. She reached over and fingered a weight that must have been the next size up, say a two-pounder. It was made of grey plastic and shaped like the larger hand weights, with a grip in the middle and bulges at both ends. The tall blonde physio grabbed the patient by his shoulders and rotated him till he had his back to her. She put one of the little beanbags in his right hand, lifted his arm and cocked it, pointing towards the ceiling at a forty-five-degree angle.

She said, 'Without moving the upper arm, stretch the forearm till the limb is straight. I'll support your elbow.' It was plain that the patient could barely manage to exercise at the one-pound level. He seemed to have no muscle tone at all. His arm shook at the elbow when he extended his forearm and hand. Such a simple movement: you might make it twenty times a day. I wondered what had happened to him; he wasn't an old man.

Then when he was struggling to hold his arm up at forty-five degrees, she moved in front of him and readjusted his fingers on the little bag. She did something that I can't describe. Slid his fingers around the bag and then made a twiddling motion with his fingers, hand to wrist.

'Try that,' she said, and while she gave him support he made the same twiddling movement with his hand. Once, then again. He looked very happy to be able to do it. Stroke victim? Onset of Parkinson's? Megan got very excited when she saw what they were doing. She popped through the open door and snatched something off the table.

'I'll bet you haven't seen this one yet,' she said to the physio. She swung her left arm up, parallel to the patient's arm and made a similar hand rotation without a weight in the hand. 'See where the forefinger positions itself? It's almost automatic. It's the natural muscle-trigger sequencing.' She put a two-pound weight in her left hand and lifted it. The physio watched her closely. 'It backs right up the arm as I lift,' Megan said. The patient lowered his arm and listened. He seemed very tired.

The physio said, 'Say, that's great. Where'd you get it?'

I was afraid she'd have to say that she'd just invented it. But not Megan; she can come up with an explanation for anything. She picked up one of the one-pound rings and slipped it on her right hand. Then she put her arm in the air and rotated the little weight in a figure-eight pattern, using her wrist and developing a rhythm while the physio watched her closely.

Megan said, 'You can keep this up almost indefinitely, for fifty to a hundred curls. Controls pain and stiffening in the fingers and wrist.'

'Actually I have seen that one before.'

Megan lowered her arm and put the weight back on the table. "I got that at the Centre for Sports Medicine. I'm there two or three times a week. I worked very closely with the physiotherapists there. You probably know most of them. They have the latest equipment.'

'Good telephone books,' said the physio.

I've been to the Centre with Megan. She really only goes there to meet guys, if you want my opinion, but while she's there she picks up all the latest talk about massotherapy, nutrition, judo, conditioning, exercise programs, medications like primidone and propranolol. There doesn't seem to be any end to it. I may have been a little jealous, because I turned to the physio and said, 'Megan hangs there; it's like being down with the 'hood, full of familiar faces that you feel like you know even if you've never spoken to each other. She took me in as her guest. It's a good place to make contacts.'

Megan grinned. 'I don't go there just to meet guys. I've got this problem with my hip joint and the sciatic nerve, and in the psoas too. I don't think my medication is helping, so we're trying to reduce the discomfort with exercise. They take time but they're positioning the hip better.'

The male patient with poor muscle tone was still standing near us, listening to the conversation. Now he said, 'Are we talking about discomfort or pain?'

Megan's face lit up; this took her into familiar territory. 'It's funny you should ask me that. We were talking about the difference only yesterday. Discomfort you can live with; it may always be there and it may tire you out, but you can function with it. You can go to work; you're mobile and so on. But when you cross over into pain you may lose some of your normal functions, movements that you take for granted. That's when you pass into medication use, wouldn't you say?'

The physio said, 'It's a very fine line; sometimes you can't tell from what a patient says exactly how much discomfort or pain he or she is experiencing?' The muscle-tone man brightened up at this. We must have been getting near his turf. 'I find it very hard to describe what I'm going through,' he said, 'and often the exercise causes more pain than the ailment. Everything I do in here makes me hurt later on. How can I know I'm making progress if I just keep hurting more and more?'

'But Mr Jackson, you've got strength and mobility now, that you didn't have four weeks ago, and muscle mass and definition. Of course you're making progress. We often have to accept pain to improve performance.'

'Well, OK to that. But is what I've got real pain or is it only discomfort?'

Megan and the physio exchanged amused looks. 'Nobody can tell you what you're feeling,' they both said at once. Then the physio said, 'No, you go first,' as if Megan was some kind of an authority.

'Well, pain, yeah,' Megan said. 'First thing, it's a fact of life these days. Everybody has to learn to live with it. Babies and little kids aren't exempt. I know a woman who runs a pain-control program that she takes around to daycares. You'd be surprised how many kids are suffering from undiagnosed headache pain.'

Mr Jackson said, 'It wouldn't surprise me one bit. Pain is everywhere. What I want to know is whether I can ever get rid of it.'

Megan looked at him and smiled. 'Stéphanie can tell you about quality of life. When we first knew each other she was doubled up, literally jackknifed, with back pain. Am I right, Steph?'

I started to say something, and then stopped. I'm not one to advertise my problems, and I couldn't have told the difference between pain and discomfort anyway. I remember the first time she took me to the Centre for Sports Medicine. I was standing beside one of the machines I needed to use, the butterfly. Pulls your shoulders back from habitual slouching. Somebody had left a twenty-five-pound disc weight on the seat. It was in my way so I looked for somebody to help me move it. I don't pick up anything that heavy. I have to be very careful my back doesn't start up. There was this guy next to me doing calf stretches. Warming up for the treadmill, I guess. I smiled at him nicely and glanced at the piece of iron, hoping he'd move it for me. He was a good-looking guy, about thirty, good pecs, tight butt. I thought it would be a breeze for him, something he could lift one-handed. But he looked up at me from his mat, and I saw he was holding a single one-pound weight.

'I'm sorry,' he said, 'I wouldn't care to risk lifting that. I have to be very careful of my sacrum, the pain, you see.'

And to look at this man, he was a perfect physical specimen. So who knows what's lurking under an appearance of health? Who can identify pain, or analyse it? Much less reduce it or banish it.

I said, 'I can function. I've got my mobility and I can cope with my job, but I've got to admit that I've never gotten rid of the discomfort. I don't believe that I ever will. What I have been able to do is to control it, and learn to live with it. I do one of my programs every night after dinner, and I take medication when the pain reaches a certain level of intensity.'

'But how can you tell when it's reached that level?'

I began to feel impatient. I mean, how can you tell about a physical feeling? There isn't any kind of fixed scale. I take Extra-Strength Tylenol when I have to. It doesn't make me constipated and I think it reduces muscular discomfort. There I go. Discomfort. I think we all feel guilty about having our pain so we prefer to call it by another name. Even discomfort seems like something to feel guilty about. We're supposed to be living in a pain-free world, where to have an ache or a pang here and there is wrong behaviour, and yet ... I don't know ... there are the rows and rows of little boxes of caps and tablets that you can get without a prescription. And every time I see a doctor he offers me something on prescription to try out and report back. There's never anything special to report. Propranolol. I can hardly pronounce it and I don't know what it's supposed to do but I take it, and it costs plenty, I can tell you, and now I wonder what may happen if I ever stop taking it. Have I built up a dependency, or to call it by another name, an addiction? We've built up a world of deadly habits for ourselves and I don't see us getting rid of it.

I will say this for the physiotherapists: they'll try almost anything before they put you on medication. That may only be because they can't legally prescribe drugs, which makes them very good about finding alternatives to drug use. I was very impressed by the way the physio in the Royal Vic handled Mr Jackson. She didn't make any extravagant promises; she didn't promise him a speedy recovery or an immediate farewell to his problems. He looked to me to be around forty-seven or forty-eight. He'd reached the point in his life when he was beginning to realize that the pain wasn't ever going to go away. He might now and then experience one of those brief moments – they come and go so fast – when he'd have a flash of what it felt like to be young in a fresh early morning – say nineteen on a fine day in June. But that would only last for a few seconds; then back would come the lassitude and the tremors and the grief, and the fear.

The physio – I never caught her name – and Megan spoke to Mr Jackson almost simultaneously. I had nothing to say to him, no new information and no promises to make, but they were ready to give him encouragement. I wish I knew why he was in the hospital. He looked all right.

'You probably can't get rid of it entirely,' they said in unison; you'd have thought they were sisters, even twins. I felt a bit left out. 'But you can do a lot to overcome it and redirect your neural and muscular responses.' Then the two of them looked at each other and laughed. 'I don't have any idea what I'm doing in here,' Megan said. 'I just popped in because I'm familiar with what you're doing.' She turned and spoke directly to Mr Jackson. 'The thing to remember is never to try too much at first. That's absolutely the worst thing you can do, and it all comes from foolish optimism. Never, never exceed what she gives in your program. If it says to do a short little five minutes on the bike, just do the five minutes, and if that makes you sweat rivers, get off the bike and acknowledge your weakness. That's the whole secret.'

'We've got to get those endorphins up and running,' said the physiotherapist. I felt suddenly as though I'd heard all this before in another context. I'm as tense as piano wire most days myself.

I thought over what they were telling Mr Jackson. It seemed like sound advice but it didn't go far enough and it didn't name names. Is discomfort another name for guilt? Isn't pain a synonym for despair? Isn't it out of control?

The Messages Are the Message

Franny finally bought a modem and it just about finished her off; it accessed telephone lines worldwide and linked her to the net, about two years ago. She didn't really understand the forces she was playing with until one evening when she happened to be glancing through a dictionary, of all things. It fell open at the definition of *modem*. *Mo*dulator/*dem*odulator. A dim notion of what might be implied in a worldwide linking of all existing databases, computers and other lines of communication began to force itself on her. She hungered and thirsted after more and more information.

She was a late arrival in the new communications; she'd lived quite happily into her mid-twenties without a personal computer. She didn't even do much keyboarding at that period. She'd have called it 'typing' and shunned it as beneath her. She was nobody's secretary, she was a researcher, employed by the university library that was about to go on-line. When it did, Franny's life changed completely.

Afterwards she remembered her sense of achievement when she used a keyboard for the first time, to bring the name and publications of her favourite author on the screen. There were more titles than the screen could display so she had to figure out unaided how to make the listings move up the surface of the screen, so as to display other material. She found the right button eventually, but not before she had to clear the display and keyboard it again. As she found her way through the instructions, she realized that she still had to copy her hard-won information into her notebook with a messy ballpoint.

After her introduction to the world of computers and information control, she proved quite adept at net-surfing, as long as it didn't imply taking dictation, which she objected to as sexist. She got quite used to popping into the catalogue rooms at the library, and punching away at the keyboards. She liked the way the screens were lighted, the neat design of the keys, and the sound everything made, a busy indescribable sound, a sound like nothing on earth.

Naturally she had to start thinking about home-computer ser-vices. She bought a few elementary instruction books and started asking around for prices, comparison shopping. At that early stage she had not begun to dream about universal information access. She may have made a costly mistake when she made a first move into the home-computer world. She bought a little laptop because she'd seen it widely advertised as a package you could carry onto commercial aircraft.

The image of herself flying business class with room for her very own computer filled her with prideful ambition. When her laptop was delivered she took a few days off work and spent them studying the manual, especially the capacity specs; she saw that her little lap-top, certainly portable and lap-sized, was very short on capacity, use-less at any but the most rudimentary level. How far did she want to take her new skills anyway? She took her little starter-computer back to the centre that had sold it to her and was told there was no market for second-hand trade-in equipment; nobody knows how many superseded computers are sitting in attics out there, but the number must be great.

So Franny went into her savings, and after consultations with cer-tain enthusiastic fellow-researchers she spent several thousand dollars on a Pomegranate 286 MB system that provided her – or so she thought – with enough storage capacity for any kind of work she intended to do. The educational network was solidly committed to this scale of equipment. The chief librarian and the instructors in research methods where she worked all claimed that the 286 was the ideal setup for most educational use. But somehow their estimate of needed capacity was rendered obsolete in the mid-1990s. Memory, memory, memory, storage capacity, more and more systems in the net … the pace of technical advance began to increase at a speed nobody could have predicted five, or even two years before. Franny began to feel wedded to information, just the very thought of it, the notion of an eternity of fact with which everybody who had the equipment could be brought into contact. Everybody might come to know everything, and everything would be happening simultaneously.

Now she bought her modem and discovered immediately that

there was no theoretical limit to the amount of knowledge, or at least information, that the device opened up to her. She accessed the Harvard library catalogue as a first venture into an enormous ocean, and clapped her hands in delight as the screen roiled and pulsed with data, more data than anyone could make use of in a lifetime of reading books. She wondered about her reading; she was spending far more time storing authors' names, and the titles of their works, than reading the actual books. Nobody could read them for her, she believed; she knew the names of more books than could be read in a dozen lifetimes. There was a certain fascination in such a state of affairs. The only limit to these pursuits was the size of her storage capacity. And soon rumours behind rumours began to reach her along the corridors of power; the library and the research institutes were about to double the size of their memories, moving to the highly sophisticated 486 MB Pomegranate package that provided functions that Franny's equipment couldn't touch.

It was then that she discovered Franny's Law. No matter how advanced your system is, there are always more advanced elements to be tied in. Stuff that you need but stuff that all has to be paid for. The institutes and the libraries could call upon public funds for the purchase of these new devices, but the purely private person had to pay for them herself. She felt betrayed. She complained about this to her friend in the chief librarian's office, a woman who had the ear of the highest authorities.

'You never told me they were thinking of making a change. Now I'm landed with an obsolete system. I can't sell it privately. Enrol me in the army of computer dupes. Even if I could find a buyer, my conscience wouldn't allow it.'

'Oh, conscience,' said the friend dismissively.

'All right, forget about conscience and find me a buyer for my 286 MB.'

'You said it yourself, Franny, it's obsolete. You'd better get a grip on yourself, young lady, and not go around making accusations. How could I guess the thing would mushroom like this?' She paused, and her eyes glazed. 'I'll tell you something else, purely for your own good. You're getting out of touch with the rest of the world. You don't even have an answering service. People don't like it when they call you and don't get an answer?'

'But they get me, if they get anything, not a machine.'

'They'd sooner talk to the machine than have to hang up.'

Franny saw that she had overlooked a crucial element of the new messaging *apparat,* the personalized answering service. Of course she would have to equip her home with such a machine. The only problems were purely technical. Which service to choose? What wording to use on her recorded message? She had friends – mostly married couples – who had taped rather oopsy greetings, sometimes in the character of their house pet, some kitty-cat, doggie, or parrot.

Hi! This is Nibbles the kitten speaking. Mommy and Daddy aren't here right now but if you'll meow your name and message they'll get back to you as soon as possible.

That was to go too far in adherence to the values of the wired world. She scripted a brief, friendly personal comment, neither cute nor coldly impersonal. Warm, engaging. These were the qualities she sought and apparently achieved. When she activated the machine in the late afternoons, on return from work, she invariably found that an ever-expanding circle of communicators had left urgent calls that had to be coped with at once.

It's Gordon, Franny. Ring me at 484-8550. I've got a nice surprise for you.

How to discourage Gordon? He was a creep in the maintenance department who seemed to be attracted to her. He kept bumping into her outside the programming wing, accidentally on purpose. Millennial men use the same strategies as their grandfathers when it comes to courtship. She decided not to return Gordon's calls, pleading excessively heavy traffic on her machine as the reason. Gordon's calls came at different hours, but always at inconvenient ones.

She hoped that her explanation would satisfy him or at least put him off, but it didn't. He kept on at her. Nice surprise, for God's sake! What was Gordon's idea of a nice surprise? The Willie Nelson CD-ROM?

A nice surprise for Franny would be an e-mail address, but nobody offered one to her; she didn't begin to get e-mail until about six months after Gordon started bugging her. Was it before she got a fax-terminal, or after? The sequence of new information became a bit blurry about this time. She would get home from the office to find four or five different classes of message waiting for her reply. Deep information lodes! Often more than a hundred and fifty individual appeals for her attention.

Ordinary mail (not so much of that any more). E-mail. Phone messages recorded on her machine. Fifty or more faxes. And now her home page, bulging with input. She could not have outlined the precise order in which these services entered her home, excepting the postal service, the earliest and much the easiest to deal with. Letters. Now and then she got a letter and sometimes (less and less often) she got a bill in the mail. Bills were much more likely to go directly and very quickly into her bank's computer. She foresaw the end of the post office as inevitable millennial flipover. Occasionally she caught herself feeling that it would be pleasant to get a letter beginning 'Dear Frances' and ending 'Love!' But not any more. Instead of loving greetings, she was buried and invisible under a mound of acronyms and screen capers, like making happy faces with the colon and open-bracket keys. Acronyms started to get into her dreams. All the states and provinces had new abbreviations, for the convenience of keyboarders who communicated fast and almost perpetually. She kept seeing FAQ, and wondered what it meant. Once she got up her courage and keyboarded in a query.

'What does FAQ mean?'

The computer replied at once, with innocent accuracy.

FREQUENTLY ASKED QUESTION.

This answer left Franny in a quandary. She typed in another question.

'I'm sure it's often asked, but what does it mean?'

The machine, sure of its ground, replied in set terms, FREQUENTLY ASKED QUESTION.

Caught without realizing in an old logical puzzle, Franny failed to understand that a name can be a thing and, as that thing, have itself for its name. It took her a while to grasp that FAQ *meant*

'FREQUENTLY ASKED QUESTION' in upper-case as well as in lower. Two grades of existence.

Then there was the further problem of identifying the computer's attitude to FAQs. Was it bored? Offended? Sulking? Finally it became clear to her that the device simply had no sense of humour; she had chums on the Internet who were convinced that it possessed all the characteristics of Divine Reason, if taken to be a single enormous intelligence possessed of wit, humour, logical acuity, pride and free will. Fifty million computers couldn't fail to generate perfect freedom and pure reason. Franny simply didn't know what to think, and her life was now at the mercy of her net connections; she had become an information addict. Her new boyfriend was a hacker in Baltimore whom she never met in the flesh until they met, by appointment, at a software conference in Cleveland.

Was it before or after they met that she installed a home fax terminal? She still spent part of each working day down at the library, but soon she would be able to carry out all the tasks of her employment contract without ever leaving her apartment, and her co-workers knew that when she fully realized this they would see no more of Franny around the cataloguing centre. She was now in full possession of the holy quartet: high-capacity personal computer, e-mail address, fax number, net service. She was among the first to discard the bogus term 'information highway' as a meaningless invention. The net was no more but no less than its participating members; it had no headquarters and no political agenda. There was nothing in the least sinister about information, its collection and retrieval. At the same time, she had an uneasy feeling that some agency or power might at any time move to exert a form of control over free exchange of data and the widening build-up of databases. This might amount to some form of censorship. It was true, she admitted, that some of the messages she received were pornographic in character and offensively personal in nature, directed to her alone. But under existing conditions you had to take the rough with the smooth. She preferred the free-ranging dirty talk to any form of data-review. There was this man in Singapore with a superbly dirty mind, who claimed to be in love with her home page.

Without any policing in place he was able to get images through to her that disgusted her when she reviewed them in her late-afternoon sessions alone at home; they also fascinated her. There was an exotic musicality about this kind of relationship; it was intensely private though carried on in front of (potentially) fifty million screens. A new take on exhibitionism and a frightening one. She didn't know where to look, but she went on looking.

Four till six in the afternoon was her big time. If she'd been down to the office she'd get home tired, turn on the answering machine, activate the fax terminal, light up her screen, and go through her mail, mostly flyers from local retailers. She was receiving information from four or five sources at once. After some time she started to wonder if perhaps she wasn't trying to know too much. There might be a condition called information underload, perhaps also ignorance.

But nobody could accuse Franny of ignorance. There might, however, be a condition or syndrome called information overload, which she might have contracted. A syndrome, she recalled, wasn't an illness like a communicable disease. It was more like a collection of symptoms for which no common source had been found. So information overload was not a syndrome. The source was clear enough; it was the range and quality of the symptoms that needed definition. What were hers? Increasing and unspecific fatigue, unreliable short memory, constant feelings of eyestrain, headache sited at the upper back of the neck, unsatisfied libido, night sweats, a sense of being a participant in some unnameable plot, of simply knowing too much without wisdom to support and interpret her facts. The woman who knew too much, she thought, and felt fear. Information overload could lead to any amount of mental distress. Now she began to fear that some unidentifiable invader had accessed her database, and was both spying on her programs and actually entering her apartment when she was away from it. Some days there were no messages on her answering machine – and that simply couldn't happen – and at other times her computer was on when she was almost sure she'd turned the thing off before leaving for the day. She couldn't be sure about this. Her memory was certainly less reliable than it had been.

Then she found herself unable to remember whether www was

in commercial competition with the original and only Internet, or simply a spinoff from it without sinister ambitions. And not too long after this lapse she came home about 3:30, a bit earlier than usual, to find that somehow or other the fax terminal had been receiving material all day. This alarmed her very much. Her living room resembled a scene in a computer animation for Disney; it had an unfamiliar aspect. She felt the muscles at the back of her knees weaken suddenly, and she plopped down on the floor and began to shed bitter tears while the fax machine went on spewing out paper, wreathing it silently around her in serpentine coils as she cried and cried.

After All!

The first time we encountered the problem was when she came to a meeting of the committee on admissions. Actually the sub-committee on admissions, which is a spinoff from the Graduate Studies Committee, doing testing, admissions, grading, counselling, review of improper procedures: these are all functions of the graduate committee as such and each function has its own subcommittee. The membership of these subcommittees is drawn from the membership of the parent Graduate Studies Committee, which has only five voting members. Am I making myself clear? You therefore tend to see the same faces on the subcommittees all the time. The department chairperson is a member of all of them *ex officio* and pretty well has to be present at every meeting of each subcommittee. It makes for a lot of work. We try to work it so that the subcommittees only meet when they have real business to take care of. The graduate committee meets regularly, once a month.

This is turning into some sort of prose-poem with the word 'committee' forming a refrain or thematic motif; that's what life in the department is like. We're all word people, discussion peddlers, coffee-shop attorneys.

Well, to get on to the problem of Molly Spencer, as I say, the difficulties started when she came to the admissions subcommittee meeting last March, when we finalized our decisions about applications for graduate study for this year. She was one of the applicants whom we'd asked to come in for a personal interview; we only do this in cases that seemed to require a personal approach. Every application gets judged strictly on merit in this department. I want to stress that. Some you can reconsider a couple of times before acceptance or rejection. The Spencer dossier was a special case, a confusing and puzzling one. I know I was confused by it. We were meeting in my office. I'm the department chair, for my sins, halfway through my second four-year term, and my office is the biggest in the department, the only one big enough to serve for committee – or subcommittee – meetings. We had the door open; the previous applicant had left ten minutes early, an easy case and a unanimous decision to accept, no debate to speak of. The four of us were beginning to wonder if this next student was going to turn up when we heard an unusual sound, a low smooth *rolling* rumble with something hypnotic about it. We hadn't heard it before but we heard it constantly from then on. She had us all hypnotized, under her spell.

What it was was she was in a wheelchair, one of those battery-powered ones that you can operate from a computerized console of buttons. They're wonderful devices, you can do anything in one. Except, of course, when the battery goes flat. I actually had that happen with Ms Spencer's chair a couple of months back, at ten o'clock on a bad February night, a Monday. It was tough to cope with, very tough. The university assists in the operation of the transport services for these people but they can't anticipate every blizzard. God, that was inconvenient. I got home at 3:30! But that is to anticipate developments.

At the admissions interview she wheeled in smoothly and positioned herself in the midst of us. I think she must have identified me as the authority figure. I'm not like that at all. I'm easily imposed on, too ready to be led by others with stronger convictions than my own. In the event, the person who felt strongest was Rina Baldwin, who never votes to reject a female applicant, no matter how borderline she may be. There are naturally some female applicants who don't quite meet the stipulated standards; that's only to be expected. But Rina resists any strict interpretation of the standards where female applicants are concerned. I've discussed this with her and she says it isn't prejudice, it's affirmative action. 'So be it' is what I say. We have to live with each other in the department after these borderline cases have done their three or four years and then gone on. WHY BE TOO INSISTENT ON STRICT STANDARDS? The loud inner voice of corruption.

The woman in the wheelchair, though, was a special case, if there are ever any real special cases. I saw from the start that it would be dreadfully inconvenient for us all to meet this one student's needs.

You would be surprised, if you haven't had to cope with them your-self, how many special needs such a person has. Molly Spencer was immobilized from the waist down. She could not walk unassisted, even the least little bit. That sounds like I was prejudiced against her admission from the start, but I really wasn't, I don't think. I could just see the problem clearly. Rina mounted her usual show of sympa-thetic advocacy, however, and the subcommittee voted to accept her, with my vote against. I believed that we didn't have the facilities to deal with this student's special needs, and that she would do better to go to a larger institution with more experience in dealing with peo-ple in her position. But more than that, I felt somehow that there was something incalculable, something fishy, about her candidacy. Well, anyway ...

In September the other students were just great with her. They were kinder to her, and more sympathetic, than the teaching staff, which frankly didn't surprise me. I and my colleagues are a bunch of hard cases, mighty set in our ways. We learned plenty last fall from our students' good-natured conduct. That's always the way.

II

Everybody who was working in the department leaned over back-wards to make things easy for this young woman. I know that's sup-posed to be patronizing. The physically challenged should be treated as nearly as possible like the rest of us. No special behaviour that might confer special privileges on a tiny minority. Fairness to all, the challenged and the unchallenged! It's a commendable ideal but it doesn't work. If you saw Molly Spencer in her chair next to a heavy fire door, trying to wrestle it open, of course you came forward to assist her, as you still sometimes might give up your seat in a bus to an elderly person or a woman burdened with parcels or carrying an infant. I think that type of act, far behind us in most instances, still occurs very occasionally. Most of the time, however, if you've got a seat on a crowded conveyance, you sit resolutely in place, rather than surrender your seat to somebody less conveniently placed.

If I held the door open for Ms Spencer, I was in a no-win situa-tion. I was patronizing her. And if I passed her by and let her go on struggling with the door I was cold-bloodedly ignoring the problems of our physically challenged associates. You can't win, but I don't suppose you have to win every time. The fact was that this student became very manipulative, insistent on rights to which she was not really entitled. The right to put her exam answers on audio cassette. Did she have any such right? Her arms were not strong enough to allow her to write out her answers to exam questions or prepare assignments. She was apparently subject to unmanageable tremors at certain times, and this made it very difficult if not impossible for her to handwrite her answers, which would have been indecipherable. We'd had other cases of students who for some reason wrote illegibly. Such students were usually permitted to type their answers to exam questionnaires, on the grounds that typed term papers were accepted routinely, so why not exam books? That was our *ad hoc*, purely practical response to a question of practice. But Ms Spencer's claim that she had a natural and legal right to present her answers vocally on cassette tape implied her further right to provide *viva voce* answers in all situations.

But all teachers know that a spoken answer to a question provides a totally different kind of response than a written answer. The written answer invariably is more detailed, specific and accurate, and less vague, than the oral reply. Orals test your presence of mind, your on-your-feet memory, your ability to speak to the point. But they never yield the same quality of information. Further to that, should we have insisted that Ms Spencer take the same amount of time to formulate her answers – in the event three or four hours – as a student writing out replies in an exam room? Her insistence on supplying us with taped answers opened up a whole range of procedural questions that we're still debating. I'm glad I'm not a constitutional lawyer. The subcommittee on review of improper procedure eventually wound up with this can of worms on the table of all its meetings. You can't anticipate the consequences of every shift in procedure. By allowing Molly to deliver her answers into the tape recorder, alone and unsupervised in her apartment, were we implying that all students should have the same right, that oral material had the same relevance and value as written? I didn't think that we were, but Rina Baldwin did. She was prepared to do away with written exams altogether, which I consider an extreme response to a specific question. A group of students in the department seized on this idea – students are normally in favour of reducing or abandoning all examination requirements – as a means of supporting Rina in her fight to do away with written tests. I see their point, of course. But I also see that a graduating doctoral candidate who has never taken a written exam will be flying on one wing for a long time after her or his degree is granted. I had no objection to the proposal's being brought into committee, and I eventually voted to allow Ms Spencer to supply taped answers to exam questions. I had my doubts but I went along. Kind of makes me think of Adolf Eichmann, that formula does. I had my doubts but I went along. I'm not sure it was a matter of fundamental principle. I can see in myself a tendency to refer every issue to fundamental principle as a kind of blocking device. If I'd gone on insisting on written answers as a matter of theoretical principle we'd never have decided on anything.

At the same time, I thought that we'd been outmanoeuvred by Ms Spencer. And very soon after this first round of debate, towards the end of the fall term, the same student raised a series of questions about her rights. Rights which were privileges in disguise if you ask me. The right to tape her answers was only the first of this series. She would claim a right to precise equality of treatment when it suited her, but also a right of special treatment when it suited her better. I'm describing what is generally called manipulative behaviour. Molly was manipulative, did we recognize its symptoms. She very much liked to have things her way; opposition invariably caused her to show her teeth. That's not the best way to put it, but my goodness, she had us all under her thumb. I must have taken her to the elevator and downstairs to the snack shop forty times in the semester, something I was glad to do, but she had other needs as well. She had to be helped upstairs to the lecture rooms and downstairs after a class to the minibus that took her home. She couldn't take notes so her professors had to speak into a microphone for her tape recorder. This altered the teachers' methods of delivery, making them over-formal and stiff in some cases, and almost inarticulate in others. I wouldn't want to have every one of my lectures taped, would you?

She had to be helped in and out of the bathroom. This was a

laborious chore but the women students were very good about it. There was a silent awareness of her gender on everybody's part. To my certain knowledge she was the cause of the termination of at least two advanced courtships. Everybody in the department seemed covertly preoccupied with Ms Spencer's physical limitations, what they allowed her, and what they denied. By early January she had become the focus of much resentment and suspicion, and a stiff test of character for all of us.

III

It's very interesting to see how 'special case' treatment breeds debate. For a minority of staff and students, Ms Spencer was getting away with murder; in the end she would receive the same diploma as themselves, for work of inferior quality. This seemed a defensible point of view, one treated by Rina Baldwin and some others as petty and illiberal. But it had a certain cogency and led certain students into questionable practices. They followed her to the minibus to make sure that she really was handicapped. One striving young man trailed the bus back to her apartment to see that she was still seated in her chair when she got home. He even went to the windows of her ground-floor apartment and reported back that they were heavily curtained but that so far as he could see she stayed in her chair while wheeling around her living room. This felt uncomfortably like spying to me, and I suggested obliquely to the student reps of the departmental council that they should discourage further attempts at surveillance; no further covert watch was attempted. It was a rotten thing to do in the first instance. And anyway, from what the original observer said, the apartment was all fitted out with aids for challenged persons, long pull cords on the blinds and curtains, low book cases with roomy shelves at floor level. Very authentic.

She arranged to get her classroom sessions scheduled to suit her in much the same style. Sometimes she was unavoidably late for a seminar, especially as winter came on and the minibus sometimes got bogged down in traffic. The loading and unloading procedure became very awkward in icy footing, and the classes couldn't start without her. She might be deprived of some important part of a discussion – to which she was entitled by right. So the other students, as many as fifteen of them, had to sit around exchanging chit-chat with the professor until the sound of the plump heavy little tires was heard approaching from the elevator. Then Molly would roll in through the door smoothly, and take her place at the front of the rows of chairs, position the microphone for her tape recorder, and give the signal to the lecturer that she was ready to tape.

This worked fairly well if the class was a lecture delivered by the professor. If it was a seminar, in which the group discussion was really very important, or if a student was giving a paper and taking questions about it – a normal form of graduate instruction – the microphone had to be passed around the room, or else the paper-reader had to sit up front beside the professor. The cord had to be disentangled from the chair legs; there was inevitably a certain amount of giggling and horseplay. Molly never became flustered or showed more than casual annoyance, but some of the other students became impatient under these special working conditions. One or two of the other women in the seminar sometimes complained openly that Molly was holding things up and interrupting the discussion. She just ignored these objections, as though she simply didn't hear them. The male students were uniformly terrified of her; she had them completely cowed. The whole undertaking was a test of everybody concerned.

IV

In the second semester, not long after Christmas, signs of resentment of the situation, even a tendency to ignore Ms Spencer's special needs, became evident, at first among the teaching staff, and afterwards among the students. I should say, for the record, that the male students were slower to show impatience than their female colleagues. Would it have been the other way around if the challenged subject had been male? I have absolutely no way of knowing. 'Gender Roles Among Physically Challenged Subjects.' A possible paper for some journal or other in the gender-studies field. Are we readier in general to assist and cooperate with persons of female gender than males? Would this be the last faint trace of what used to be called chivalry? It was never the exclusive property of males, only when women were chivalrous we called it by different names: kindness, compassion. These qualities came to have a bad reputation with feminists, along with male chivalry, which is simply horseplay with a fancy name.

One bad-tempered winter afternoon about the end of January or the beginning of February – I remember it was Saturday – I was down in the McGill Métro station, approaching the entry to the Bay at the east end of the platform. My eye was caught by a figure a short distance off, a trimly built, long-striding person, female, in the winter clothing of a contemporary woman in her mid-twenties, denim trousers, I recall, and a leather jacket. She was moving briskly and strongly; she was outdistancing me. We were both headed for the doors of the Bay.

The set of this woman's head, neck and shoulders, and something in the way she moved, seemed oddly familiar. I speeded up, meaning to catch up to her and offer friendly greetings, the way you do at a chance encounter on a subway platform. As she drew near the big pair of doors at the end of the station, I suddenly realized that what I had spotted was the top half of Molly Spencer, her head and neck, shoulders, arms and back. Everything below her waist was unrecognizable because totally unfamiliar. I moved up closer to get a better look at her. I was astounded to see her like this, in perfect control of all her movements, able to walk or run as well as me, or better.

I was close behind her when we came close to the entryway. I think she must have seen my reflection in the glass doors, because she suddenly took off through the entrance and away to the right, through the men's-wear department. I kept her in sight, and she knew it. She curled around to the left, beside a long rack of winter overcoats. She doubled past me on my left, heading back to the doorway we'd just come through. She nipped out onto the Métro platform; by the time I got through the doors she was halfway down the platform, heading for Eaton's. Once she got in there she'd be gone. With all the tunnels and boutiques in there you could hunt her for days without a hope of catching her. I broke all records very quickly for the distance from the Bay to Eaton's, and actually caught up with her just as she flung a door open to enter Eaton's. She had no difficulty with the door; she had no visible tremor. So I grabbed her by the shoulder and turned her around to face me, whereupon a security guard appeared at once, primed to bear witness to a case of sexual harassment.

'Is this man bothering you, Madame?'

'Don't interfere,' I said to him crisply, 'just get a police officer in here immediately. I want to bring a charge.' The security man let his mouth fall open, gasped, then turned and made off for the elevator bank, none too speedily. I reckoned it would be a while before he got back – if he ever did. I held on to Ms Spencer tightly. It was like trying to land a big slippery fish, perhaps a tarpon. I don't know why I think of a tarpon. I know nothing about fish or fishing.

She wriggled energetically in my clutch.

'Let me go, you fool,' she spat at me. 'What are you going to charge me with? I've done nothing wrong.' She slapped at me with her free arm; there was considerable force in the blow, and it stung.

By this time a considerable crowd had collected, none of them showing any sympathy with me; there were grumblings of protest at my behaviour. I felt intimidated. I looked at the growing mob and saw that I would never be able to convince then that this energetic person had perpetrated a criminal imposture.

'Fraud,' I said to her, feeling my clutch weaken. 'You're an impostor.'

'Nothing of the kind,' she said, looking to the crowd for support, 'I've just been doing some research for a sociology thesis on the lifestyles of the physically challenged. If I want to live in a wheelchair, I've a perfect right to do so.' She certainly was no sociologist.

'But … but …' I sputtered, 'you've been such a hell of a nuisance.'

'And you've all been such kind liberal ladies and gentlemen, haven't you? You're the frauds if anybody is.'

I released her arm and stepped gingerly away from her. I could see an overweight policeman pushing through the crowd. I was in a no-win situation. I was checkmated. I watched her disappear without trying to keep my hold on her, and I got out of there quickly. I didn't want to become entangled with the Montréal police, a peculiar body of men. What could I have said to them? Technically, I suppose, she had committed no offence. She hadn't profited from her impersonation, as far as I could see, not in any way you could put your finger on. Maybe she just liked being in the chair, who can say? But I mean, really, after all!

Checklist

'Bit Parts'. Final draft: September 28 – September 29, 1991.

'Assault of the Killer Volleyballs'. Final draft: October 27 – October 29, 1991. Published in *Carousel* no. 9 (University of Guelph, 1993).

'Swedes in the Night'. Final draft: November 22 – November 23, 1991.

'Too Much Mozart'. Final draft: December 21 – December 22, 1991.

'The Bug in the Mug'. Final draft: August 30 – August 31, 1992.

'Life in Venice'. Final draft: September 27 – September 30, 1992.

'Plumbers'. Final draft: November 5 – November 6, 1992.

'A Subject for Thomas Hardy'. December 15 – December 19, 1992.

'Deconstruction'. Final draft: October 19 – October 23, 1993. Published in *Carousel* no. 10 (University of Guelph, 1994).

'A Gay Time'. Final draft: November 14 – November 21, 1993.

'A Catastrophic Situation'. Final draft: December 11 – December 14, 1993.

'There Are More Peasants Than Critics'. Final draft: September 13 – September 18, 1994.

'How Did She Find Out?'. Final draft: October 9 – October 11, 1994.

'Finishing Together'. Final draft: December 15 – December 20, 1994.

'Pain Control'. Final draft: November 16 – November 23, 1996.

'The Messages Are the Message'. Final Draft: November 26 – December 5, 1996.

'After All!'. Final draft: December 7 – December 15, 1996.

Hugh Hood was born in Toronto in 1928 and studied at the University of Toronto, where he completed his Ph.D. in 1955. He worked as a university teacher for over forty years – over thirty of those years spent at the Université de Montréal. He was married to painter and printmaker Noreen Mallory and had four children. He died in Montreal in August of 2000.

Hood wrote 32 books, amongst them novels, collections of stories and essays, an art book, and a book of sports journalism. His most extended project, begun in 1975 and occupying him right up until the time of his death, was a twelve-volume *roman fleuve* entitled *The New Age/Le Nouveau siècle*. The last book in this series, *Near Water,* was published by Anansi in 2000.